THE SKY WAS FALLING ON THEM . . .

Then Marco turned the ship and there, surrounded by a transparent shell, was the flat Earth.

"This set-up must take vast amounts of power," Kin gasped. "The sun's orbit is all wrong. What keeps the seas from emptying? Why have they got their own private stars when there's real ones out there—"

"It looks as though the big sphere is only transparent from the outside," Marco said. "We can see in, they can't see out."

"How could we get in?" Kin asked. Marco grimaced.

Twenty minutes later, they hovered over the hole. "Don't breathe," said Marco. "We're going in."

"That's easy," he said. "I saw a hole in the shell."

Their ship dropped through the hole with a few meters to spare, and the proximity detectors shrilling. They were still going mad when Kin looked up and saw a ship speeding toward them. It hit in one of the holds and sent the sky wheeling crazily . . .

STRATA

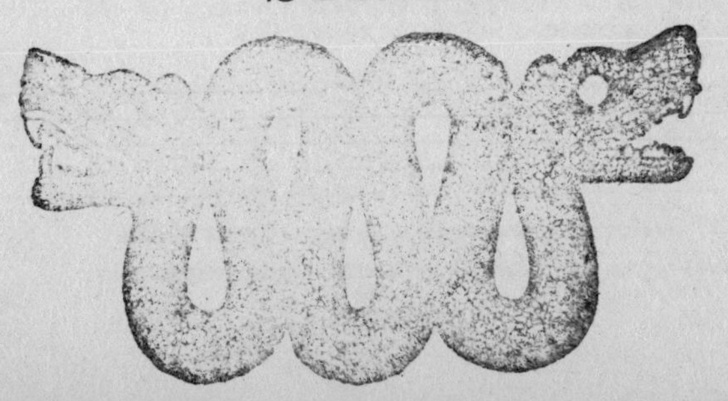

Strata

by
Terry Pratchett

A ROC BOOK

ROC
Published by the Penguin Group
Penguin Books USA Inc., 375 Hudson Street,
New York, New York 10014, U.S.A.
Penguin Books Ltd, 27 Wrights Lane,
London W8 5TZ, England
Penguin Books Australia Ltd, Ringwood,
Victoria, Australia
Penguin Books Canada Ltd, 10 Alcorn Avenue,
Toronto, Ontario, Canada M4V 3B2
Penguin Books (N.Z.) Ltd, 182–190 Wairau Road,
Auckland 10, New Zealand

Penguin Books Ltd, Registered Offices:
Harmondsworth, Middlesex, England

Published by Roc, an imprint of Dutton Signet,
a division of Penguin Books USA Inc.

Published by arrangement with St. Martin's Press, Inc.

First Printing, March, 1983
10 9 8 7 6 5 4

REGISTERED TRADEMARK—MARCA REGISTRADA

Printed in the United States of America

BOOKS ARE AVAILABLE AT QUANTITY DISCOUNTS WHEN USED TO PROMOTE PRODUCTS OR SERVICES. FOR INFORMATION PLEASE WRITE TO PREMIUM MARKETING DIVISION, PENGUIN BOOKS USA INC., 375 HUDSON STREET, NEW YORK, NEW YORK 10014.

I met a mine foreman who has a piece of coal with a 1909 gold sovereign embedded in it. I saw an ammonite, apparently squashed in the fossil footprint of a sandal.

There is a room in the basement of the Natural History Museum which they keep locked. Among other oddities in there are the tyrannosaurus with a wristwatch and the Neanderthal skull with gold fillings in three teeth.

What are you going to do about it?

Dr. Carl Untermond
The Overcrowded Eden

It was, of course, a beautiful day—a Company brochure day. At the moment Kin's office overlooked a palm-fringed lagoon. White water broke over the outer reef, and the beach was of crushed white coral and curious shells.

No brochure would have shown the nightmare bulk of the pontoon-mounted strata machine, the small model for islands and atolls under fifteen kilometers. As Kin watched, another meter of beach spilled out of the big back hopper.

She wondered about the pilot's name. There was genius in that line of beach. A man who could lay down a beach like that, with the shells just right, deserved better things. But then, perhaps he was a Thoreau type who just liked islands. You got them sometimes; shy silent types who preferred to drift across the ocean after the volcano teams, dreamily laying complicated archipelagoes with indecent skill. She'd have to ask.

She leaned over her desk and called up the area engineer.

"Joel? Who's on BCF3?"

The engineer's lined brown face appeared over the intercom.

"Guday, Kin. Let me see now. Aha! Good, is it? You like it?"

"It's good."

"It's Hendry. The one who's the subject of all those nasty depositions you've got on your desk. You know, the one who put the fossil dino in—"

"I read it."

Joel recognized the edge to her voice. He sighed.

"Nicol Plante—she's his mixer—she must have been in on it too. I put them on island duty because, well, with a coral island there is not the temptation—"

"I know." Kin thought for a while. "Send him over. And

her. It's going to be a busy day, Joel. It's always like this at the end of a job—people start to play around."

"It's youth. We've all done it. With me it was a pair of boots in a coal measure. Not so imaginative, I admit."

"You mean I should excuse him?"

Of course he did. Everyone was allowed just one unscripted touch, wasn't he? Checkers always spotted them, didn't they? And even if one went unnoticed, couldn't we rely on future paleontologists to hush it up? Huh?

Trouble was, they might not. . . .

"He's good, and later on he'll be great," said Joel. "Just gnaw one ball off, eh?"

A few minutes later Kin heard the machine's roar stutter and stop. Soon one of the outer office robots came in, leading—

—a squat fair-haired youth, tanned lobster pink, and a skinny bald girl hardly out of her teens. They stood staring at Kin with a mixture of fear and defiance, dripping coral dust onto the carpet.

"All right, sit down. Want a drink? You both look dehydrated. I thought they had air conditioning in those things."

The pair exchanged glances. Then the girl said, "Frane likes to get the feel of his work."

"Well, okay. The freezer's that round thing hovering right behind you. Help yourself."

They jerked away as the freezer bumped into their shoulders, then grinned nervously and sat down.

They were in awe of Kin, which she found slightly embarrassing. According to the files they were both from colony planets so new the bedrock had hardly dried, while she was manifestly from Earth. Not Whole, New, Old, Real or Best Earth. Just Earth, cradle of humanity, just as it said in their history books. And the double century mark on her forehead was probably something they'd only heard of before joining John Company. And she was their boss. And she could fire them.

The freezer drifted back to its alcove, describing a neat detour around a patch of empty air at the back of the room. Kin made a mental note to get a tech to look at it.

They sat gingerly on the float chairs. Colony worlds didn't have them, Kin recalled. She glanced at the file, gave them an introductory glare, and switched on the recorder.

"You know why you're here," she said. "You've read the regulations, if you've got any sense. I'm bound to remind you that you can either choose to accept my judgment as senior executive of the sector, or go before a committee at Company HQ. If you elect for me to deal with it, there's no appeal. What do you say?"

"You," said the girl.

"Can he speak?"

"We elect to be tried by you, Mizz," said the boy in a thick Creed accent.

Kin shook her head. "It's not a trial. If you don't like my decision you can always quit—unless of course I fire you." She let that sink in. Behind every Company trainee was a parsec-long queue of disappointed applicants. *Nobody* quit.

"Right, it's on record. Just for the record, then, you two were on strata machine BVN67 on Julius Fourth last, working a line on Y-continent? You've got the detailed charge on the notice of censure you were given at the time."

" 'Tis all correct," said Hendry. Kin thumbed a switch.

One wall of the office became a screen. They got an aerial view of gray datum rock, broken off sharply by a kilometer-high wall of strata like God's own mad sandwich. The strata machine had been severed from its cliff and moved to one side. Unless a really skilled jockey lined it up next time, this world's geologists were going to find an unexplained fault.

The camera zoomed in to an area halfway up the cliff, where some rock had been melted out. There was a gantry and a few yellow-hatted workmen who shuffled out of camera field, except for one who stood holding a measuring rod against Exhibit A and grinning. Hi there, all you folks out there in Company Censure Tribunal Land.

"A plesiosaur," said Kin. "All wrong for this stratum, but what the hell." The camera floated over the half-excavated skeleton, focusing now on the distorted rectangles by its side. Kin nodded. Now it was quite clear. The beast had been holding a placard. She could just make out the wording.

" 'End Nuclear Testing Now,' " she said levelly.

It must have taken a lot of work. Weeks, probably, and then a very complicated program to be fed into the machine's main brain.

"How did you find out?" asked the girl.

Because there was a telltale built into every machine, but that was an official secret. It was welded into the ten-kilometer output slot to detect little unofficial personal touches, like pacifist dinosaurs and mammoths with hearing aids—and it *stayed* there until it found one. Because sooner or later everyone did it. Because every novice planetary designer with an ounce of talent felt like a king atop the dream-device that was a strata machine, and sooner or later yielded to the delicious temptation to pop the skulls of future paleontologists. Sometimes the Company fired them, sometimes the Company promoted them.

"I'm a witch," she said. "Now, I take it you admit this?"

"Yarss," said Hendry. "But may I make, uh, a plea in mitigation?"

He reached into his tunic and brought out a book, its spine worn with use. He ran his thumb down it until the flickering pages stopped at his reference.

"Uh, this is one of the authorities on planetary engineering," he said. "May I go ahead?"

"Be my guest."

"Well, uh. 'Finally, a planet is not a world. Planet? A ball of rock. World? A four-dimensional wonder. On a world there must be mysterious mountains. Let there be bottomless lakes peopled with antique monsters. Let there be strange footprints in high snowfields, green ruins in endless jungles, bells beneath the sea; echo valleys and cities of gold. This is the yeast in the planetary crust, without which the imagination of men will not rise.' "

There was a pause.

"Mr. Hendry," asked Kin, "did I say anything there about nuclear-disarmament dinosaurs?"

"No, but—"

"We build worlds, we don't just terraform planets. Robots could do that. We build places where the imagination of human beings can find an anchor. We don't bugger about planting funny fossils. Remember the Spindles. Supposing the colonists here turn out like them? Your fossil would kill them, blow their minds. Docked three months labor. You too, Miss Plante, and I don't even want to know for what reasons you were helping this nitwit. You may go."

She switched off the recorder.

"Where are you going? Sit down. All that was for the benefit of the tape. Sit down, you look dreadful."

He was no fool. She saw the embryo hope in his eyes. Best to scotch that now.

"I meant it about the sentence. Three months enforced vacation. It's on the tape, so you won't talk me out of it. Not," she added, "that you could."

"But we'll have finished this job by then," he said, genuinely hurt.

Kin shrugged. "There'll be others. Don't look so worried. You wouldn't be human if you didn't yield to temptation. If you feel bad, ask Joel Chenge about the boots he tried to lay down in a coal seam. They didn't ruin his career."

"And what did you do, Mizz?"

"Hmm?" The boy was looking at her sidelong.

"You sort of give the impression I've done something everyone else has done. Did you do it too?"

Kin drummed her fingers on the desk. "Built a mountain range in the shape of my initials," she said.

"Whee!"

"They had to rerun almost half a strip. Nearly got fired."

"And now you're Sec-exec and—"

"You might be too one day. Another few years they might let you loose on an asteroid of your very own. Some billionaire's pleasure park. Two words of advice: Don't fumble it, and never, *never* try to quote people's words against them. I, of course, am marvelously charitable and understanding, but some other people might have made you eat the book a page at a time under threat of sacking. Right? Right. Now go, the pair of you. For real this time. It's going to be a busy day."

They hurried out, leaving a coral trail. Kin watched the door slide across, staring into space for a few minutes. Then she smiled to herself, and went back to work.

Consider Kin Arad, now inspecting outline designs for the TY-archipelago:

Twenty-one decades lie on her shoulders like temporal dandruff. She carries them lightly. Why not? People were never meant to grow old. Memory surgery helped.

On her forehead, the golden disc that multiple centenarians often wore—it inspired respect, and often saved embarrassment. Not every woman relished attempted seduction by a man young enough to be her great-to-the-power-of-seven grandson. On the other hand, not every elderly woman wore a disc, on purpose. . . . Her skin was presently midnight-black, like her wig—for some reason hair seldom survived the first century—and the baggy black all-suit.

She was older than twenty-nine worlds, fourteen of which she had helped to build. Married seven times, in varying circumstances, once even under the influence of love. She met former husbands occasionally, for old times' sake.

She looked up when the carpet cleaner shuffled out of its nest in the wall and started to tidy up the sand trail. Her gaze traveled slowly around the room as though seeking for some particular thing. She paused, listening.

A man appeared. One moment there was air: the next, a tall figure leaning against a file cabinet. He met her shocked gaze, and bowed.

"Who the hell are you?" exclaimed Kin, and reached for the intercom. He was quicker, diving across the room and grabbing her wrist politely yet agonizingly. She smiled grimly and, from a sitting position, brought her left hand across and gave him a scientific fistful of rings.

When he had wiped the blood out of his eyes she was looking down at him and holding a stunner.

"Don't do anything aggressive," she said. "Don't even breathe threateningly."

"You are a most unorthodox woman," he said, fingering his chin. The semisentient carpet cleaner bumped insistently against his ankles.

"Who are you?"

"Jago Jalo is my name. You are Kin Arad? But of course—"

"How did you get in?"

He turned around and vanished. Kin fired the stunner automatically. A circle of carpet went *wump.*

"Missed," said a voice across the room.

Wump.

"It was tactless of me to intrude like this, but if you would put that weapon away—"

Wump.

"There could be mutual profit. Wouldn't you like to know how to be invisible?"

Kin hesitated, then lowered the stunner reluctantly.

He appeared again. He *wiped* himself solid. Head and

torso appeared as though an arm had swept over them, the legs popped into view together.

"It's clever. I like it," said Kin. "If you disappear again I'll set this thing on wide focus and spray the room. Congratulations. You've managed to engage my interest. That's not easy, these days."

He sat down. Kin judged him to be at least fifty, though he could have been a century older. The very old moved with a certain style. He didn't. He looked as though he'd been kept awake for a few years—pale, hairless, red-eyed. A face you could forget in an instant. Even his all-suit was a pale gray. As he reached into a pocket, Kin's hand moved up with the stunner.

"Mind if I smoke?" he said.

"Smoke?" said Kin, puzzled. "Go ahead. I don't mind if you burst into flame."

Eyeing the stunner, he put a yellow cylinder into his mouth and lit it. Then he took it out and blew smoke.

This man, thought Kin, is a dangerous maniac.

"I can tell you about matter transmission," he said.

"So can I. It's not possible," said Kin wearily. So that was all he was—another goldbricker. Still, he could turn invisible.

"They said that it was impossible to run a rocket in space," said Jalo. "They laughed at Goddard. They said he was a fool."

"They also said it about a lot of fools," said Kin, dismissing for the moment the question of who Goddard was. "Have you got a matter transmitter to show me?"

"Yes."

"But not here."

"No. There's this, however." He made a pass and his left arm disappeared. "You might call it a cloak of invisibility."

"May I, uh, see it?"

He nodded, and held out an empty hand. Kin reached out and touched—something. It felt like coarse fiber. It might just be that the palm of her hand underneath it was slightly blurred, but she couldn't be sure.

"It bends light," he said, tugging it gently out of her grip. "Of course, you can't risk losing it in the closet, so there's a switch area—here. See?"

Kin saw a thin, twisting line of orange light outlining nothing.

"It's neat," said Kin, "but why me? Why all this?"

"Because you're Kin Arad. You wrote *Continuous Creation*. You know all about the Great Spindle Kings. I think they made this. I found it. Found a *lot* of other things, too. Interesting things."

Kin gazed at him impassively. Finally she said, "I'd like a little fresh air. Have you breakfasted, Jago Jalo?"

He shook his head. "My rhythms are all shot to hell after the trip here, but I think I'm about due for supper."

Kin's flyer circled the low offices and headed northward to the big complex on W-continent. It skirted the bulk of what had been Hendry's machine, its new pilot now laying down a pattern of offshore reefs.The maneuver gave them an impressive view of the big collector bowl atop the machine, its interior velvety black.

"Why?" said Jalo, peering. Kin twirled the wheel.

"Beamed power from orbiting collectors, slaved to the machine. If we flew over the bowl we wouldn't even leave any ash."

"What would happen if the pilot made a mistake and the beam missed the bowl?"

Kin considered this. "I don't know," she said. "We'd certainly never find the pilot."

The flyer skimmed over some more islands. Vat-bred dolphins, still frisky after their journey in the megatanker, looped through the waves alongside its shadow. Blast *Continuous Creation*!

But at the time it had seemed a good idea. Besides, she had done just about everything else but write a book. The actual writing hadn't been difficult. The real problem had been learning how to make paper, then hiring a staff of robots and setting them to building a printing press. It had been the first book printed in four hundred years. It had caused quite a stir.

So had the words inside the expensively produced card covers. They said nothing new, but somehow she had managed to assemble current developments in geology in such a way that they had struck fire. According to reports the book had even been the basis for a couple of fringe religions.

She looked sideways at her passenger. She was unable to trace his accent—he spoke meticulously, like someone who had just taken a learning tape but hadn't had any practice. His clothes could have been bought out of a machine on a dozen worlds. He didn't look mad, but they never did.

"So you've read my book," she said conversationally.

"Hasn't everyone?"

"Sometimes it seems so."

He turned red-rimmed eyes to her.

"It was okay," he said. "I read it on the ship coming here. Don't expect any compliments. I've read better."

To her disgust Kin felt herself reddening.

"No doubt you've read plenty," she murmured.

"Several thousand," said Jalo. Kin kicked the flyer onto automatic and spun around in her seat.

"I know there aren't even hundreds of books; all the old libraries are lost!"

He cringed. "I did not mean to offend."

"Who do—"

"It isn't necessary for an author to make the paper," said Jalo. "In the old days there were publishers. Like filmy factors. All the author did was write the words."

"Old days? *How old are you?*"

The man shifted in his seat. "I can't be precise," he said. "You've changed the calendar around a few times. But as near as I can make out, about eleven hundred years. Give or take ten."

"They didn't have gene surgery in those days," said Kin. "No one is that old."

"They had the Terminus probes," said Jalo quietly.

The flyer passed over a volcanic island, the central cone fuming gently as a tech squad tested it out. Kin stared at it unseeing, her lips moving.

"Jalo," she said. "Jalo! I thought the name was familiar! Hey . . . the big thing about the Terminus ships was that they would never come back. . . ."

He grinned at her, and there was no humor in it. "Quite correct," he said. "I was a volunteer. We all were, of course. And quite mad. The ships were not equipped to return."

"I know," said Kin, "I read a filmy. Ugh."

"Well, you've got to see it against the background of the times. It made a kind of sense, then. And of course, my ship didn't come back."

He leaned forward.

"But I did."

* * *

The Ritz was in the unofficial city that had grown up around what had been the first and was now the last Line. Now even the city was breaking up, being towed back up the wire to the big freighters in orbit. In another month the last Company employee would follow it. The last snowfield would have been laid. The last hummingbirds would have been released.

Their conversation on the roof garden of the restaurant was punctuated by the slap and rattle of yellow tugs climbing the Line two kilometers away, towing strings of redundant warehouses like beads on a wire. They were soon lost in the cirrus, bound for Line Top.

Kin had ordered framush, saddleback of loom and breasens. Jalo had read the menu intently and had ordered, in frank disbelief, a dodo omelette. He looked now as though he regretted it.

Kin watched him pick at it, but her mind persisted in showing her pictures. She remembered the bell-shaped bulk of a Terminus probe, the pilot's life system a tiny sphere at the tip. She remembered the frightening logic that had led to the building of the monsters. It went like this:

It was far better to send a man into space than a machine. In the complete unknown, a man could still evaluate and decide. Machines were fine for routine, but they flipped when presented with the unforeseen.

It was cheap to send a machine because it did not breathe and it sent its information back alone.

Whereas a man breathed, all the time. This was expensive.

But it was very cheap to send a man if you did not arrange to bring him back.

"Is that celery in the jug?" said Jalo.

"It's snaggleroot shoots," said Kin. "Don't eat the yellow bits, they're poisonous. Now, do I have to sit here waiting? Speak to me," she murmured, "of the Great Spindle Kings."

"I only know what I read," said Jago. "And most of what I read, you wrote. Can I eat these blue things?"

"You've found a Spindle site?" Only nine Spindle sites had been found. Ten, if you included the derelict ship. The prototype strata machine had been found on one. So had the details of gene surgery. No wonder more people studied paleontology than engineering.

"I found a Spindle world."

"How do you know it's Spindle?"

Jalo reached over and took some snaggleroot.

"It's flat," he said.

It was possible, Kin conceded.

The Spindles had not been gods, but they would do until gods showed up. They had evolved on some light world . . . possibly. The surviving mummies certainly showed them to be three meters tall but weighing only ninety pounds. On worlds as heavy as Earth they wore marvelous exoskeletons to prevent themselves collapsing with multiple fractures. They had long snouts, and hands with two thumbs, legs banded alternately in orange and purple and feet big enough for a circus clown. They had no brain, or, to be more precise, their whole body could act like a brain. No one had ever been able to find a Spindle stomach, either.

They didn't look like gods.

They had cheap transmutation but not FTL travel. Possibly they had sexes, but exobiologists had never found out where little Spindles came from.

They sent messages by modulating a hydrogen line in the spectrum of the nearest star.

They were all telepaths and *acute* claustrophobes. . . . They didn't even build houses. Their spaceships were . . . unbelievable.

They lived nearly forever, and to while away the time they visited planets with a reducing atmosphere and played with them. They introduced mutated algae or oversized moons. They force-bred lifeforms. They took Venuses and made Earths, and the reason, once you accepted that Spindles were different, made sense at least to humans. They were spurred by a pressing population problem—pressing, that was, to Spindles.

One day they had ripped up a planetary crust with a strata machine and found something dreadful—dreadful, that was, to Spindles. In the next two thousand years, as the news spread, they died of injured pride.

That was 400 million years ago.

A tug plunged down the Line, the braking roar leaking through its sonic screen. The Line marshals were cutting the loads adrift a few thousand miles up and sending them on their way by strap-on rocket, to keep Line weight down.

The tug swung through the switching system and hummed off toward the distant marshaling yards. Kin looked at Jalo with narrowed eyes.

"Flat," she said, "like an Alderson disc?"

"Maybe. What's an Alderson disc?"

"No one ever built one, but you hammer all the worlds in a system into a system-wide disc with a hole in the middle for the sun, and you plate the underside with neutronium for gravity, and—"

"Good grief! You can work neutronium now?"

Kin paused, then shook her head. "As I said, no one's ever built one. Or found one."

"This one is not much more than thirteen thousand miles across."

Their gazes met. She rolled out the word he was waiting for.

"Where?"

"You'll never find it without me."

"And you think it's a Spindle artifact?"

"It's got things you'd never believe in a million years."

"You intrigue me. What is your price?"

For an answer Jalo fumbled in a belt pouch and brought out a wad of 10,000-Day bills. Company scrip was harder than most world currencies. Any one of them represented almost twenty-eight years of extended life if cashed at a Company trading post. The Company's credit was the best. It paid in extended futures.

Without taking his gaze off Kin, Jalo summoned the nearest robot waiter and pushed a handful of bills into its disposal hopper. Every instinct cried out to Kin to leap up and grab them back, but even with science on your side one did not live past the first century by obeying instincts. The automatic incinerator would have burned her hand off.

"How . . ." she croaked. She cleared her throat. "How juvenile," she said. "Forgeries, of course."

He handed her a methuselah bill, the highest denomination issued by the Company.

"Two hundred and seventy years," he said. "A gift."

Kin took the gold-and-white plastic. Her hands emphatically did not tremble.

The design was simple, but then there were more than two hundred other tests for the authenticity of Company scrip. *Nobody* forged it. It was widely advertised that any hypothetical forgers would spend all the years that had been fraudulently manufactured in the Company vaults, passing them in novel and unpleasant ways.

"In my day," said Jalo, "I would have been called rich, rich, rich."

"Or dead, dead, dead."

"You forget I was a Terminus pilot. None of us really believed in the inevitability of our death. Few people do. I have been proved right so far. In any case, you are welcome to test the bill. It is genuine, I assure you.

"I have not come to buy. I want to hire *you*. In thirty days I'm returning to the . . . flat world, for reasons that will become obvious. I intend to be away less than a year, and the pay I offer is the answers to questions. You may keep that bill, of course, even if you do not accept. Perhaps you would like to frame it, or maybe keep it for your old age."

He vanished like a demon king. When Kin lunged across the table her hands met empty air.

Later she ordered a check on all shuttles going up the Line. Not even an invisible man could have got past the telltales secreted in the gangways. He'd hardly attempt to board a freight shuttle—most were not even pressurized.

He didn't. Kin realized later that he had bought a ticket under an assumed name and just walked past the security net, flaunting his visibility like a cloak.

The message came twenty-five days later, along with the first wave of colonists.

The main Line had long since gone, winched up into its synchronous-orbit satellite and loaded aboard a freighter. There were still a few cosmetic teams just finishing work at the antipodes.

Around Kin, as she stood on a knoll in the midst of the tangled jungle, the steaming, scent-encrusted land was bare of any obvious human mark. Eight thousand miles under her feet, she knew, men, robots and machines were converging on and boiling up the antipodal wire; soaring into the last of the freighters, a twelve-mile skeleton with one big fusion motor, and leaving the world to the newcomers.

Despite appearances, it would be a planned withdrawal. Last off would be the sweepers, carefully scuffling over the ruts. A Company publicity film had once shown the last man off being winched up a few feet on the Line, then bending back to brush out his footprints. Not true, of course—but it missed the truth by mere inches.

It was a good world. Better than Earth, but they said now that Earth was improving—population up to nearly three-quarters of a billion now, and that didn't include too many robots.

Better than her childhood. Kin had long ago dispensed with most of her early memories in a periodic editing, but she had kept one or two. She winced as she recalled the oldest.

A hill like this one, overlooking a darkening countryside wreathed in ragged mists, and the sun sinking. Her mother had taken her there, and they stood in the small crowd that was the total population of almost half of a country. Most of them were robots. One of them, a Class Eight, hide crisscrossed with repair welds, lifted her onto its shoulders for a better view.

The dancers were all robots, although the fiddler was human.

Thump, thump went the metal feet on the dark turf, while early bats hunted for insects overhead.

The steps were perfect. How could they be otherwise? There were no men to hesitate or stumble. The world was too full of things for the few humans to do that they should concern themselves with this. Yet they knew that such things must be continued against the day men could once again pick up the reins. Back and forth, crossing and leaping, the robots danced their caretaker Morris.

And young Kin Arad had decided then that people should not become extinct.

It had been a near thing. Without the robots, it would have been a certainty.

While the stamping figures rocked darkly against the red sunset sky, she made up her mind to join the Company. . . .

The first of the big gliders swept over the trees and touched down heavily on the grass. It slammed into a tree, spun around and stopped.

After a few minutes a hatch slid back and a man stepped out. He fell over.

Kin watched him haul himself up and lean back into the hatch. Two other men came out, followed by three women. Then they saw her.

She had taken pains. Now her skin was silver and her hair black, shot with neon threads. She had chosen a red cloak. In the absence of wind, electrostatic charges kept it floating about her in a sufficiently impressive way. No sense in skimping details. These people were coming to a new world. They had probably already drawn up a proud constitution writ in gold and freedom. They ought to be welcomed with dignity. There would be too much time later for reality.

More gliders were drifting down, and the man who had been the first to step out climbed up to Kin on her knoll. She noticed his pioneering beard, his chalk-white face. But most of all she noticed the silver disc on his forehead, glinting in the first rays of sunlight.

He topped the rise still breathing evenly, pacing himself with the effortless self-control of most centenarians. He grinned, exposing teeth filed to points.

"Kin Arad?"

"Bjorne Chang?"

"Well, we're here. Ten thousand of us today. You make some good air—what's the smell?"

"Jungle," Kin said. "Fungi. Decaying pumas. Purple scents from the flowers of hidden orchids."

"You don't say. Well, we shall have to see about that," he replied evenly.

She laughed. "I'm frankly surprised," she said. "I had expected some jut-jawed young fellow with a plow in one hand . . ."

". . . and a model constitution in the other. I know, I know. Someone like that headed up the colony on Landsheer. Did you hear about Landsheer?"

"I saw pictures."

"Did you know they spent a week arguing about forms of government? And the first thing they built was a church. And then the winter hit them. And I've been up there in the northern continent in the winter. You make your winters cruel."

Kin started to stroll down, Chang loping along beside her.

"We did not want them to die," she said at last. "We told them about weather patterns."

"You didn't tell them that the universe is *unfair*. They were too young to be properly paranoid."

"And you?"

"Me? I think even *I'm* out to get me. That's why these people have hired me. I'm going on one hundred and ninety. I don't want to die, so I will watch the weather like a hawk, and only swim in shallow water, and eat nothing until I've seen a complete laboratory analysis. I'll even duck in case of meteorites. I've got a five-year contract down here, and I intend to survive it."

Kin nodded. His self-confidence reassured even her.

But she also knew it wasn't quite so simple. In theory, the older you grew the more careful you were to stay near a gene surgery and the local Company store, where your Days could be cashed for carefully calculated longevity treatment—at the guaranteed rate of twenty-four standard hours extra life per Day. Only the Company paid in Days, and only the Company gave the treatment. Textbook economics followed that the Company owned everywhere and everybody.

But textbook economics also spoke of the law of diminishing returns. At twenty you acted circumspectly, taking no risks, because if you worked for the Company you had centuries ahead of you. A shame to throw them away by fast driving or high living.

At two hundred, who cared? You'd been everywhere, done everything. All new experiences were just old experiences, rearranged. By three hundred you were probably dead. Not quite by suicide, however—not quite. You just climbed higher and higher mountains, or free-fell higher and longer, or backpacked across Mercury the difficult way, and sooner or later the odds ran out.

Boredom drove you frenetic. Death was Nature's way of telling you to slow down.

That's why Chang led a party of greenhand colonists to a new world. There was really nothing to lose except a life stretched thin by endless living.

"We don't build pleasure planets," said Kin. "You'll have to win this one."

A glider drifted overhead and was lost among the treetops.

"They'll hate it first," said Chang. "That thing's got all the supplies in it, the blankets and the dumbwaiters. I told control to land it ten miles away. It's a nice day. A walk will do us good, and we can see who is the type to tread on poisonous spiders."

"What will you do when the five years is up?"

"Oh, I don't know, probably stay and become the Grand

Old Man for a while. Anyway, by then I'll have this place too civilized for my own comfort."

"Hmm? Reme wasn't built in a day."

"I wasn't a foreman on *that* job."

The colonists were watching her silently. No gene surgery, no treatment, no Company store—yet they had volunteered. Not one in ten of them would see a century.

They would have the immortality granted to simple people. There would be children. There were few enough children now, even on Earth. Genes would survive, while conditions on this world worked their own surgery on them. Hammered on the anvil of a different sun and moon, in a thousand years the people here would be *different*. Just different enough, according to the Plan.

"Here's where we say goodbye," said Kin, reaching for the pouch at her belt. "Here's the Deed, the conveyance and a five-thousand-year warranty against faulty construction."

Chang pushed the documents into his shirt.

"Have you thought of a name?" Kin asked.

"The vote went in favor of Kingdom."

Kin nodded. "I like it. Simple, but not jokey. Maybe one day I'll be back to see how well you work, Mr. Chang."

The last glider down was a Company carrier, in contrast to the cheap vermifoam of the disposable pioneer machines. As Kin walked toward it the hatch opened and a Company robot let down the steps.

"When did you last have the treatment?" said Chang suddenly. Kin stared at him.

"Eight years ago. Should it matter?"

He paused, and moved closer so that the crowd couldn't hear.

"The Company's in trouble. Perhaps our Days are numbered?"

"Trouble?"

The robot pilot registered that Kin was aboard, counted three seconds, and slid the door. The last the pioneers saw of Kin was her perplexed face in the big rear port as the machine drifted away and up.

Chang watched until it was high enough to use the ramjets. Then he reached into the hatch of his own glider, and lifted out a megaphone.

The crowd became a smudge, a dot, and lost itself in the

jungle. Kin sat back. The Company owned 60 percent of infinity. What trouble?

Soon the glider overtook the sun, which set in a reverse dawn. Later they landed on a small sandy island, white in the starlight, surrounded by phosphorescent seas.

The Line was black against the sky. At its base was one small capsule, and a man leaning against it.

"Joel!"

He grinned his Neanderthaler grin. "Hi, Kin."

"I thought you'd gone to be a Sector Master on Cifrador."

He shrugged. "I was offered it. Didn't suit me. Come aboard. Robot!"

"SAH!"

"Hook the glider on tow."

"SHO NUFF, SAH!"

"And knock off the slave talk, will you?"

They climbed up to the Linesman's cabin and sat down on either side of the central traction tube. Joel Chenge sighed and flicked a switch. There was a jolt, and Line started to flow hypnotically past them as the capsule climbed.

"I'm the new Watcher here," he said.

"Oh, Joel! Surely not?" Kin had a sudden feeling that the bottom was dropping out of the universe.

"Surely yes. Just between ourselves, I'm rather looking forward to it. Wouldn't you?"

"But I can't see you—" Kin stopped.

—you, she meant, spending centuries in a deep-freeze cabinet on a high-orbit satellite of this world. Never growing older. She could picture it, and it was horrible.

Robot waldoes hovering eternally with syringes held a few inches from the ice-hard skin, while other robots watched the world below. Looking for certain signs. Fission. Fusion. Space flight. High power use.

Some worlds made space flight a prime target, hoping to achieve early interstellar recognition. It never worked. Even suborbital machines were the apex of a pyramid, huge and old, resting on things like subsistence agriculture. It was no good trying to fly before you could eat.

Joel leaned over and punched up a meal on the console dumbwaiter, which extruded a laden table. He caught Kin's eye and grinned again. Joel often grinned. Paleolithic genes had somehow met again at his conception, and a slab face like Joel's had to smile frequently lest it frighten small children. When his face brightened it was like the dawn of Man. They spoke, and not merely with words. Between them they were four hundred years old. Now words were mere flatcars on which towered cargoes of nuance and expression.

Kin looked down at the table again.

"It's familiar," she said. "Uh, I'm trying to remember—"

"One hundred and thirty years ago. We got married, remember? On Tynewalde. There was that mad religion—"

"Icarus Risen," said Kin suddenly. "Hell, I'm sorry. And you even remembered the menu. How romantic."

"Actually, I had to look it up in my diary," he said, pouring the wine. "Were you my fifth wife? I neglected to make a note."

"Third, wasn't it? You were my fifth husband."

They looked at one another and burst out laughing.

"Good times, Kin, good times. Three happy years."

"Two."

"All right, two. Good grief! That time on Plershoorr, wasn't it, when we—"

"Don't dodge. Why a Watcher?"

The temperature fell like collapsium. Beyond the cabin windows Kingdom was turning from a landscape to a disc, sunlight driving the terminator ahead of it.

"Uh. Life gets a bit stale. On treatment alone I'd never live as long as a Watcher: nice to see a new world grow; see what the future holds; it'll be as good as visiting a new universe—"

"You're gabbling, Joel. I know you, remember? I've never known you bored. I recall you spending two years learning how to make a wooden cartwheel. You said you'd never rest till you had mastered every skill. You said you never learned to spear a seal, or cast copper. You said you were going to write the definitive work on robot pornography. You haven't, yet."

"Okay. I'm ducking out because I'm a coward. Is that good enough? Things are going to happen soon; best place'll be in a freeze box."

"Things?"

"Trouble."

"Tro—" She paused. "Chang said that."

"The big pioneer? I talked to him yesterday, when they

were all in orbit. He's getting out before the storm breaks too."

"What are you talking about?"

He told her. Kin had reported the visit of Jalo. She had also reported his ability to produce high-denomination Day notes.

"The Company examined that methuselah bill you sent in, Kin."

"A forgery."

He shook his head slowly. "Wish it had been. It was—sort of genuine. Only we didn't print it. The numbers were all wrong. All the codes were wrong. Not inaccurate, you understand. It was just that they aren't our numbers. We haven't issued those numbers yet.

"Now think about it. There's a process for duplicating Company currency. Think what that means, Kin."

She thought about it.

Company scrip was subject to so many hidden checks and codes that any forgery would *have* to be a duplication. And you couldn't duplicate a Day bill even by running it through the works of a strata machine, because the Company owned all the machines and one hidden key in every thick plastic note would fuse the whole thing. *No one* could duplicate Company currency. But if they could—

Multiple-centenarians would be the first to suffer. Company scrip was so reliable it was wealth in its own right. But if Day bills were just bits of plastic, if the market was flooded with ten or twenty times the real amount—the Company wouldn't exist. Its wealth was its credibility, and its credibility was the hardness of its currency.

Gene surgery merely stopped you dying. You could go on living without the additional treatments that Days would buy, but you would grow old. Immortal, but senile.

No wonder they were hiding out. Joel was grabbing a sort of immortality, Chang was at least escaping the crash. Probably the less level-headed were doing things like taking a space walk without a suit.

There must be millions of us, Kin thought. We complain about never eating a dish we haven't eaten before and the colors slowly draining out of life. We wonder if the shortlifers live more vividly, and dread learning that they do because we gave up the chance of children. It would be so unfair. As if a man has only a certain allocation of things like elation and delight and contentment, and the longer he lives the more they must be diluted.

But life is still sweet and death is just mystery. It is age we dread. Oh hell.

"Did they look for him?" she said.

"Everywhere. We know he's been to Earth, because all the Terminus probe records in the Spaceflight Museum have been wiped clean."

"Then we know nothing about him at all?"

"Right. Find a bolthole, Kin." He gave a short laugh. "At least Company policy was right. Our worlds will last."

"One man can't bring down a civilization," said Kin.

"Show me where it says that's a universal rule," he snapped, and then relaxed. "This cloak . . . *really* invisible?"

"We-ell, if you looked directly, I remember things behind it being just slightly blurred. But you wouldn't notice if you weren't expecting it."

"Useful for old-fashioned espionage, maybe," mused Joel. "Very odd, though. I don't think we would make one. You have to have a pretty high technology for that sort of thing, and in a high technology invisibility wouldn't be a very great asset. So many other things would detect you."

"I wondered about that," said Kin.

"Then all this about matter transmission—all the theories say it isn't quite possible. The Wasbile double effect almost does it, the same way you can always build an almost-perpetual motion machine."

The satellite at the Line's end was a bright star ahead. Joel glanced down the controls.

"I'd have liked to have met him," he said. "I read about the Terminus probes when I was a wee lad. Then once when I was on New Earth I went to see Rip Van LeVine's farm. He was the one who landed on the planet and found—"

"I know about him," said Kin.

If Joel had noted the tone in her voice—and surely he must have—he didn't show it. He went on cheerfully. "Couple years ago I saw this film they made on the T4 and T6. They're the ones who are still traveling. There's a charity on New Earth, every ten years or so they put a couple of ships on a flick-orbit to build up acceleration and—"

"I know about that, too," said Kin.

The ships built up acceleration by diving into New Earth's sun, then making an Elsewhere jump back a few million miles, then diving, then jumping . . . and finally popping out of nowhere a few hundred light-years away at a light-squashing speed and a few miles from the probes.

Terminus Four hadn't decelerated at turnover point, and a fault in Six's primitive computer had guided it precisely to a star that wasn't there. In the normal course of events the pilots would have decomposed centuries ago. Suspended animation had been pretty primitive then, too. But the ailing machinery had long ago been piecemeal-replaced, and the visiting crews added refinements every decade or so.

It wasn't cheap. It would have been a lot easier to thaw out the pilots and bring them back to a life of luxury. But Rip Van LeVine, the death-and-glory Terminus pilot who after a thousand-year voyage landed on a world settled by Elsewhere-driven ships three hundred years previously, had been a rich man when he suicided. Rich enough to employ good lawyers, and to insist that his trust do everything that could be done for the last two pilots—except wake them.

"The LeVine Trust has us tied in knots," said Joel. "The first thing the Company thought of was to wake the T4 pilot and ask her about Jalo. They all trained together, so she might know something. But apparently the whole of New Earth would raise hell if we tried it."

"Joel, what do you think of that idea?" said Kin.

He met her gaze. "I think it's despicable, what else?"

"So do I."

She stayed at the satellite until Joel had finished setting the system, and watched while he activated the circuit that broke the long-chain artificial molecule that was the Line. Now Kingdom was on its own.

She didn't stay to watch him ready the freeze room.

Her private boat had been left in orbit near up. Technically she was on leave until she joined the rest of the team at Trenchert, where the advance parties had already cleaned the atmosphere and strengthened the crust. Months ago she had planned to stop off at Momremonn-Spitz for a look at the new Spindle excavations there. There had been rumors of another working strata machine.

Right now it seemed less than important. She slammed the airlock's inner door shut behind her.

"Salutations, lady," said the ship. "The sheets are aired. We are fully fueled. Shall we run you a bath?"

"Uhuh."

"We have the course computed. Do you wish a countdown?"

"I think we can dispense with all that excitement," said Kin wearily. "Just run that bath."

When the ship boosted the bathwater slopped gently against the edge of the tub, but did not spill. Kin, who had been brought up to be polite to machines, said: "Neat."

"Thank you. Five hours and three minutes to flickover."

Kin soaped an arm thoughtfully. After a few minutes she said: "Ship?"

"Yes, lady?"

"Where the hell are we going? I don't recall giving you any instructions."

"To Kung, lady, as per your esteemed order of 338 hours ago."

Kin rose like a well-soaped Venus Anadyomene and ran through the ship until she dropped into the pilot chair.

"That order," she said softly, "repeat it." She watched the screen intently, one hand poised over the panel that would open a line back to Kingdom Up. Joel wouldn't have frozen himself yet, the process took hours. Anyway, a machine could just unfreeze him. The important thing was that the station had a big enough transmitter to punch a message through to the Company. She recognized the touch of Jago.

The transmitted order had been simple enough, prefaced by the ship's call sign and Kin's own code. It had come over the normal ground-to-orbit channels. It could have come from a dozen transmitters while work on Kingdom was being completed.

It had ended: "A flat world. You, Kin Arad, are a very curious person. Cheat me and you will forever wonder what sights you missed."

Kin's hand dropped—and didn't touch the message switch.

You *couldn't* build a flat world.

But then, you *couldn't* come back if you were a Terminus pilot.

And you *couldn't* duplicate Company scrip.

"Ship?"

"Lady?"

"Continue to Kung. Oh, and open a channel to the screen in my study."

"Done, lady."

It was wrong. It was probably foolish. It would certainly get her fired.

Be there or forever wonder.

She filled the hours by relearning Primary Ekung and reading the supplements to the planetary digest. It appeared the kung now had a Line, but no one had got around to banning ship landings on the world itself. Nothing much was banned on Kung, even murder. She checked and found it was now the only world in local space that actually allowed ships to land under power. Was that relevant?

Kung was hungry for alien currency. There wasn't a great deal Kung could produce that humans could use, except a whole variety of pneumonia-type illnesses, but there was a lot Kung wanted. It was trying to start a tourist industry. . . .

Kin had been there. She recalled rain. The kung had forty-two different words for rain, but that just wasn't enough words to encompass the great symphony of water that fell for fifty-five minutes in every hour. There were no mountains. The light gravity had allowed plenty to rise, but it allowed lots of ocean spray into the wind to wash them down. The nubs that remained had a dispirited, back-turned look.

Of course, sometimes they became islands. Kin remembered about the tides.

An overlarge moon and a cool, close sun meant nightmare tides. Vegetation was either fungal, able to spring up and fruit hurriedly at low tides, or it was resigned to a semisubmerged life.

And tourists came. Even though they had to wear float jackets most of the time in case of flash tides, the tourists came. They were fishermen and mist enthusiasts, mycophiles and *Wanderjahr* biology students. As for the kung themselves . . .

She switched off and sat back.

"You should have told the Company," she said silently. "There's still time."

She answered: "You know what will happen. He might

be mad, but he's no fool. He'll be prepared for any trap. Besides, Kung isn't a human world. Company writ runs thin down there. He'll duck and weave and we'll lose him."

She said: "You have a duty. You can't let a menace like him run around loose just to satisfy your curiosity."

She answered: "Why not?"

How rich is Kin Arad, daughter of the genuine Earth and author of *Continuous Creation* (*q.v.*)? The Company paid its servants in Days, but since they could earn far more than a Day in a day, they often sold surplus time for more traditional currencies. Temporally, then, her account showed that she had another three hundred and sixty-eight years, five weeks and two days in hand, plus one hundred and eighty thousand credits—and a credit is worth a credit these days.

In any case, credits were backed by Days. The galaxy had rare elements in plenty. The transmuter at the heart of every strata machine or dumbwaiter could make anything. What else but longevity itself could back a currency? Kin could buy life. Could Solomon have done it? Could Cloritty have done it? Could Hughes have done it?

She was rich.

An alarm bleeped. Kingdom's sun bulked in the forward screen as a fire-rim black disc, the sensors having long ago been appalled by its brightness.

Kin switched off the ship's voice, because she hated the countdown to an Elsewhere jump. It was like waiting for death. If the computer was right, and it was never wrong, the ship would jump just as soon as it was at an acceptable orbital speed with regard to—

(a few seconds of vertigo, a brief agony of despair. Soul-lag, it was called on little evidence. Certainly *something* in the human mind refused to travel faster than—it had been experimentally verified—0.7 light-years per second, so that after even a short jump through Elsewhere space there was a hollow black time before the rushing mental upwellllll—)

—the destination world. Kin caught her balance, and looked out. The Kung sun was a cool red dwarf. Statistics said it was small. They lied. From four million miles away it was a giant. Kung practically rolled through its upper atmosphere—and there it was, a perceptible black disc. Kin smiled. Kung, living under permanent cloud cover, were mad enough to begin with. What sort of religion would they have developed if they had been able to see the sky?

Three hours later she left the ship a few miles from Kung Line Top.

The satellite was decorated in Kung style—gray and brown-purple predominated, with startling touches of heart-attack red. There was no immigration control. Kung welcomed smugglers. Smugglers were rich.

Her suit's jets wafted her gently into one of the airlocks, which cycled automatically.

Line Top! The spaceward end of the monomolecular wire that linked every civilized world with the greater galaxy! The gateway to the stars, where robots jostled with ten-eyed aliens, spies moved circumspectly, golden-bearded traders of strange and subtle wares sold curious powders that made men go mad and talk to God, and cripple boys played strange electronic instruments that plucked emotions. Line Top! A hefty kick and you had escape velocity. Line Top! Threshold of the universe!

Anyway, that was the idea. But this was reality, and Kung was in a poor time for the tourist trade. The kung that loped through the tethered satellite's corridors were admittedly colorful, but familiar. There *was* a unipodal Ehft operating a sweeping machine in one corridor. If it was a spy for the Galactic Federation, it was a master of disguise.

The big board on the main concourse said there was an hour to wait until the next downward shuttle. Kin found a bar with a window overlooking the shuttle hall. The bar was called the Broken Drum.

"Why?" she asked the kung behind the bar. Saucer-eyed, he fixed her with the bland stare of barmen everywhere.

"You can't beat it," he said. "Your wish?"

"I thought kung had no sense of humor."

"That is so." The bar-kung looked at her carefully. "From Earth?" he asked.

"Yes," said Kin.

"Which one? I've got a brother-uncle on Real Ea—"

"The genuine one," said Kin sharply. He looked at her thoughtfully again, then reached under the counter and pulled out a filmy cassette that Kin recognized with a sinking heart.

"I thought the face was familiar," said the bar-kung triumphantly. "Soon as you walked in, I thought, very familiar face—of course it's a bad holo on the filmy, but still . . . Ha. Do you think you could do a voice print on it, Miss Arad?" He grinned horribly.

She smiled valiantly, and took the tape translation of *Continuous Creation* from his damp four-fingered hands.

"Of course, it's not for you, I understand, it's for your nephew Sam." She murmured cruelly. The kung looked startled.

"I have no nephew Sam," he said, "although I had intended it for my son-brother Brtkltc. How did you know?"

"Magic," sighed Kin.

She took her drink to the big window, and idly watched tugs shunting cargo shuttles across the marshaling wires while behind her she half-heard the bar-kung talking excitedly to someone on the intercom. Then a someone was standing by her chair. She looked around, and then up. A kung was standing beside her.

Look at the kung. Seven feet tall, and then topped off with a red coxcomb that was made of something like hair. Two saucer eyes filled the face, and they were now two-thirds closed against the lights that had been turned up by the bar-kung out of deference to Kin. The body was skeletal, with body-builder's muscles strung like beads on a wire and a bulge between the shoulder blades for the third lung. The shipsuit it wore was a masterpiece of tailoring. It had to be. The kung had four arms.

It grinned. A kung grin was a red crescent with harp strings of mucus.

"My name is Marco Farfarer," he said, "and if it will help you to cease staring, I am a naturalized human being. You only think you're seeing a kung. Don't let a mere unfortunate accident of birth confuse you."

"My apologies," said Kin. "It was the second pair of arms."

"Quite so." He bent lower, and said in the voice laden with the breath of swamps, "A flat world?"

Then he sat down, while they sought for clues in each other's face.

"How did you know?" said Kin.

"Magic," he said. "I recognized you, of course. I enjoyed your book. I know Kin Arad works for the Company. I see her sitting in Kung Line Top, a place one would not expect to find her. She looks ill at ease. I recall that about a month ago, when I was on Ehftnia and couldn't get a ship out—being only the third-best long-haul pilot in the region—I was approached by a man who—"

"I think I know the man," said Kin.

"He said certain things and made certain offers. What did he offer you?"

Kin shrugged. "Among other things, a cloak of invisibility."

The kung's eyes widened. "He offered me a small animal-skin pouch which produced these," he murmured. Kin picked up the notes he laid on the table. There was a wad of 100- and 1000-Day bills, an Ehftnic ceramic 144-pjum bar, a thin roll of assorted human currencies, several hundred Star Chamber tokens and a computer card.

"Some of the currency I tendered to a moneychanger on Ehftnia," said Marco, "and she accepted it. There can be no greater proof of its genuineness, if you have ever done business with an Ehftnic. I think the card is a keycard to an autobank, probably an Ehftnia.

"There was a lot more, mostly Ehftnic dollar bars. I was poor at the time."

Kin flicked a pjum bar and watched it roll across the table.

"The bag produced them?" she asked slowly.

"Aye. 'Twas no more than hand-sized. I watched it all come out. I thought he was Company. He wished to buy my services."

"As a pilot?"

The kung waved two hands vaguely. "I can fly all kinds of ship, no error. Even without matrix tapes. I'm the best— What do these want?"

The bar-kung approached the table diffidently towing behind him a very large hairy bell, which kept up by hopping on its one foot. There was a voicebox strapped to the tuft of its tip.

"This is Green-shading-to-indigo. It's an Ehft," he said, helpfully. "It's the Line Top Sanitary Officer."

"Pleased to make its acquaintance," said Kin. With a deft flick the Ehft produced a transparent box from under its—cloak, skin?—and flourished it a few inches in front of Kin's eyes. She heard Marco hiss.

"*Voilà! Regardez!*" screeched the voicebox. "Earthian! Moutmout! Sapient! Question!"

A large black bird in the box looked beadily at Kin, and went back to preening its feathers.

"It turned up yesterday," said the bar-kung. "I told him, it's a bird, an Earth animal. Only it talks.

"We looked it up in the *Guide to Sapient Species*, but there is only one avian, and this is not it."

"It looks like a damn big raven," said Kin, taking the box. "What's the problem?" She paused. "I see the problem. You want to know, do you arrest it or destroy it? Anyway, how did a bird get in here?"

"Puzzle!"

"We don't know."

On an impulse Kin opened the box. The bird hopped up onto the rim and looked at her.

"It's harmless," she said. "Probably someone's pet."

"Pet?"

"Mentalsymbiote," drawled Marco. "Humans are crazy."

The Ehft shuffled forward uncertainly and shoved its tentacle toward Kin again. It held a thick loop of intricately knotted string. With a sinking heart she recognized it as an Ehftnic touch-book.

"When I told it you were you, it went all the way back to its pod for its translation of your book," said the bar-kung proprietorially. "It wants you to—"

But Kin was already tying a personalized knot at the beginning of the coil.

"Understand! Not! Self!" squawked the voicebox. "For! Pup! Belong! Sibling!"

"He means—"

"I understand," said Kin wearily.

"Jalo," screamed the raven.

"You take it away," said the bar-kung, thrusting the "cage" into a pair of Marco's arms. "She can feed it or eat it or make love to it or teach it to sing or whatever humans do with pests."

"Pets," said Marco. He took the cage. There didn't seem to be any alternative.

The Ehft watched them head toward the shuttle bay.

"Crazy?" it ventured.

"Humans run the Universe now," said the bar-kung bitterly. "Such craziness, I wish I could get hold of some. Notice the way humans walk as if they own the galaxy?"

The Ehft considered this. It had always found it an effort to comprehend a method of locomotion that didn't involve tentacles.

"No," it said.

There were few passengers on the shuttle. There was a moment of high-gee as strap-on rockets sent it swinging out of the hangar and down the Line.

"At least I'll have a native guide," said Kin, and grinned to show that it was a joke. But this kung seemed to know about humor. *Legally* human?

"I was hoping you might be able to help me there," said Marco, fishing a pouch out of his traveling bag. "I've never been down there in my life. Sometimes I've run freighters here, but only as far as Up."

"You mean you got that close and never went to look at your people's world?"

"Whose people's world? I was born on Earth."

He brought out a bone-colored pipe, filled it from a pouch and lit it with an everglow. Kin wrinkled her nose.

"What'n hell's that?"

"Tobacco," said Marco. "Cutty Peerless VI. There's a man in London sends it out to me. That's London England, you understand."

"Do you enjoy it?" There was a click as the cabin air filters came on. Marco took the pipe out of his mouth and looked at it reflectively.

"On the whole, no," he said, "but it is historically satisfying. May I ask you a question?"

"Go right ahead."

"Do you have a thing about kung? Sexually, I mean?"

Kin stared into the great gray eyes and at the mottled skin, and the snappy answer died in her throat. She recalled occasional rumors. Marco radiated maleness from his matchstick figure. Kung males were almost unbelievably masculine. And priapic, apparently. Kung were directly polarized, male and female, with none of that subtle elision between the absolute male and absolute female psyches that humans possessed. To some human women the kung machismo was magnetic.

"Never in a thousand years," she said levelly. "You can call me old-fashioned if you like."

"Thank goodness," said the kung. "I hope I did not cause offense?"

"Nothing that won't heal. What, er, made you ask?"

"Oh, you wouldn't credit the stories I could tell you, Kin Arad. Of young human females with *Freffr*-comb hairstyles and what they think is genuine kung-style dress and a superficial and uninformed taste in *Tleng* music. When I played piano in a nightclub on Crespo during the spacer slump I had to lock my windows at night, and once two young—" He paused, then went on. "Of course, I realize you are a cosmopolitan woman. But I once had to hit the wife of a New Earth ambassador with a chair."

The raven fretted in its transparent cage. Kin glanced at it.

"What are we going to do if Jalo contacts us?" she said.

Marco took the pipe out of his mouth. "Do? I intend to visit this flat world. What else?"

Tide was up when the shuttle juddered into the terminal, smoke pouring from the brake pads. The kung had solved the water-level problem by building the terminus buildings on a raft that rose up and down the line as the migrating oceans shifted around the planet.

Kin peered out into the gray rain. Around the station raft other woven buildings were bobbing at their anchor poles. A few kung were abroad this early, paddling coracles along the shifting streets like a regatta for Gollums.

Marco splashed up, dragging a small and terrified kung behind him.

"This says it's been hired to pick us up. Not very dramatic, is it?"

Prodded by Marco, the boatkung led them over the gaggle of boats moored around the platform to a human-built tourist speedster, its four balloon tires now doubling as flotation bags. Kin settled into the back seat. The rain was warm, and she was already sodden. Maybe there was something particularly penetrative about kung water.

Marco shoved the boatkung into the front passenger seat and fumbled with the controls. The mooring rope groaned and parted as the boat bucketed forward between wings of spray.

He drove with three arms draped nonchalantly over the seat.

Four arms. Four arms were rare. In the bad old days before the Revolution, high-caste kung had used mitogenetic techniques to influence the growing embryo. Four arms meant warrior caste. Kin decided to try tact.

"How come," she asked, "how come you have to have your shirts specially made?"

He didn't look around. "Family tradition," he said. "My family always sent one male into the warriors, and they operated on my mother, but—you remember the Line Break of '58?"

"Sure. Earth was cut off for a month. Some lunatic bombed both termini simultaneously."

"Yes. My parents were on the embassy staff at New Stavanger. By the time the Line was replaced my mother was in labor."

And the kung believed that when a child was born it's receptive mind was taken over by the nearest available discarnate soul. . . .

"As a matter of fact my father was prevented from killing himself by the Shand cultural attaché, who was dining with him," said Marco levelly. "He thought he could get to me first, you see? It didn't work. So they put out humanity papers on me and found me a home with an old couple down in Mexico, and then they left Earth. End of story. How come you're bald?"

Kin's hand flew to her wig.

"Uh. Age. Hair can't take it."

Marco was watching the horizon intently. "Oh," he said. "I wondered. I always think one shouldn't be shy about this sort of thing, don't you?"

The boat chattered through half-drowned groves and flotillas of villages until it was brought to a dead halt by weeds brushing against the hull. Marco swore, and kicked the power changeover.

"It's the tide," said Marco. Hull out of water, they whirred on through streaming vegetation. A few late fish, abandoned by the water, were hopping awkwardly after the departing sea. On Kung only amphibians survived for long.

Presently the vegetation and the gradient suggested country that was seldom inundated for more than one hour in twenty. Under the boatkung's direction they picked up a track that wound up into permanently dry grassland. If Kung had been a human world it would have been cultivated to within an inch of its life. The kung shunned it as a desert.

The boat jolted over a ridge.

There was a round valley, with the inevitable lake at the bottom, a spaceship bobbing at its center.

"It's a General Motors Neutrino, ground-to-ground ring-rim fusion motor, Spindle unibrake, thirty-four staterooms, choice of extras," said Marco, lighting his pipe. "The in-system systems are a bugger. I flew one once. They were built to meet a demand which wasn't."

It looked like a fat doughnut.

"Has it got any armaments?" asked Kin weakly.

"Jalo!" screamed the raven.

"Wouldn't like to be on the wrong side of the fusion flame."

The boatkung was looking at Marco's pipe in terror. "Apart from that—there's a roomy hold. Name your own horrors."

As they stepped into the ship's open hatch the boatkung gunned his craft and headed back across the lake.

"Looks like the only way off is up." said Kin. "I wonder what frightened him?"

"Me," said Marco, and walked aboard soundlessly—then hissed and crouched into a fighting stance.

A shape lurched toward them. Racial memories told Kin to run and climb a tree. The *thing* bearing down on them could only be intent on clawing gashes in soft membranes, and gouging with those fangs. Racial memories were behind the times, as usual. Kin grinned politely.

The shand could just about stand in the high corridor without its tiny ears touching the ceiling, which meant it was almost three meters high. It was, though, holding the knee-sagging, self-effacing posture that shandi always adopted inside the artifacts of smaller races, as if in terror lest they accidentally eat someone.

Typically, it—she—was as broad as she was high, with wide arms ending in calloused knuckles that could double as another pair of feet. There was an intelligent bear's face, but it was a bear with binocular vision and a domed skull and several walruses in its ancestry. It had two tusks, said to have been used originally for scraping mollusks from the beds of freezing oceans, now as useless as the vermiform appendix, and carved into status-denoting shapes. Its snout—

"If you have klite fliniffed?" she lisped reproachfully.

There was something altogether familiar about some of those tusk carvings. Kin stuck her fingers in the corners of her mouth for tuscal effects and tried her Shandi.

"I am Relative/Almost-Parched-and-Dry and the kung is—Small-stain-go-far," she spat. "I greet you in all grease, O shand of the Lower Conwexi Delta Moraine Region, unless I am very much mistaken."

"I congratulate you on your mastery of the Speech," said the shand graciously. "My name is fifty-six syllables long, but you may call me Silver. Are you coming to the flat world? Is the kung dangerous? He looks uneasy."

"I think it's because he can't understand Shandi. On the other hand, all kung look uneasy. It's probably something to do with the flash tides. This one's human, by the way; don't press the point."

"What are you talking about?" Marco asked suspiciously.

By the time Silver had led them into the ship's observation cabin they had reached a compromise. Kin and Marco spoke to Silver in allspeak, which the shand understood but, because of her tusks, could not speak; Silver spoke in shandi, which she could pronounce and Marco could not understand; and Kin translated into allspeak for Marco. Eventually it was established by careful retranslation that Silver was a sociologist, comparative historian, linguist and meat-animal herder.

"All of them?" asked Marco.

"I once knew a shand who was an elevator attendant, biochemist and seal hunter," said Kin.

"I got here yesterday," said Silver. "I was working on Prediquac when this man—"

"We know him," said Kin. "What did he offer you?"

"I do not understand," said Silver blankly.

"Bait," said Kin. "To go with him to the flat world."

"Oh, I see. Nothing. Should he have done?"

Kin translated. Marco stared at the shand in astonishment, then snorted and wandered off into the depths of the ship.

"There is something familiar about your name," said Silver to Kin.

"I wrote a book called *Continuous Creation.*"

Silver smiled politely. "Did you?"

Marco had disappeared. The two females took a stroll through the doughnut hull. With every step Kin became more uneasy. This was a *strange* ship.

It had been converted to a freighter. There were four staterooms. The rest of the torus was fuel tank.

The ship had been designed to be a rich idiot's toy. Only rich men and spies used ships that could stagger out of a gravity well under their own power.

Consider: There was a Line on every useful world, and once up the Line all that was needed was a pressurized box with altitude jets and an Elsewhere matrix to get you to the top of any other Line. A few specialized trades and the tourist industry used ships capable of traversing a solar system. There were even some ships that could fly ground-to-orbit in an emergency. *No one* needed a ship that could reach orbit *and* fly across a system *and* jump via the Elsewhere.

This one could. Kin's unease began to be tinted with excitement. The Line and the Matrix had chopped space into mere pauses between identical Line Top arrival lounges. This ship was something else.

There was a dumbwaiter, a big model programmed to produce anything from lobster thermidor to sawdust. It could even produce shand proteins.

There was a medical room that would not have disgraced a city. There was also a deep freeze, a fact so unusual that Kin lifted the lid.

"Now here's a thing," she murmured. Silver peered in, and rooted around among the frosted packages.

"Nothing remarkable," she said. "Meat, fish, fowl, leaves, swollen tubers—human food."

Kin pointed at the dumbwaiter, humming seductively to itself.

"Ever known one of those to fail?" she said.

"They don't," said Silver. "If they did, you humans would never have allowed us into space."

"Then why waste space and weight hauling this junk? If he was nervous, he'd bring shandi food—uh. Of course. I forget he's *old.*"

"Old?"

"Old enough to be fussy about machine-made food. This lot here must have cost him a fortune."

"Please explain about 'old,' " said Silver insistently.

Kin told the shand about the Terminus probe. When she finished she was aware that the giant was looking at her oddly.

"You humans must have been *mad* for space," she said.

They turned as Marco strode silently into the room, trembling with rage.

"What is this ship?" he bawled. "There's enough weaponry in the hold to blow a hole through a planet."

"And small arms," murmured Kin. Marco stared at her, while she felt her mind beginning to think very fast indeed.

"Precisely. But how did you guess?"

"No guess. I think I've seen enough. Silver, was there a message from Jalo when you got here?"

"The kung in the ferry said I was to wait. Why?"

Kin shook her head urgently. "Marco, there must be spacesuits around. If we got into them, could you evacuate the ship?"

"Down here? It'd implode. I'd have to take her up, and that—"

"This is a .0003 Clipe automatic. If you all leaped at me the chances are I would not get you all, but who could I shoot first?"

Jalo was standing by the door, the pistol dangling nonchalantly from one hand. Kin thought about what a stream of Clipe needles could do, and decided to stand very still. She glanced at Silver.

The shand wasn't looking at Jalo. She was staring at Marco.

He had dropped into a curious bowlegged stance, arms held out from his body like an ancient gunfighter, and he was hissing softly.

"Tell it if it attacks, I will shoot," said Jalo. "Tell it!"

"You know he can understand you," said Kin coldly. She heard Silver say in shandi: "In a minute there's going to be an almighty fight, Kin. No one threatens a kung and lives."

"Marco is legally human," said Kin in allspeak.

"Yes, that fooled me," said Jalo. "I should have known better. I told that agency computer on Real Earth to pick three people that fitted my specifications, and it gave me three names. The damn thing never bothered to say two of them were BEMs."

Only Silver, student of history, understood the term. She growled.

"It surely mentioned planets of origin," said Kin.

"The big frog was born on Earth, though, and the bear born in a ship orbiting Shand," said Jalo. "Doesn't anyone ever mention *species* these days? Legally human! Ye gods! *Do not move.*"

"I was wondering where you were," said Kin. "I should have been looking for a patch of fuzzy air—*looter*."

He grinned lopsidedly. "The word is, uh, nasty but true. Just as the Company looted stata machines and the Line monomolecular technique."

"Not true. The Company administers them for the general good."

"Fine, so on this trip the profits will be for my general good. I figure I'm owed something. I knew LeVine and the rest. I trained with them. I'm taking my reward now. I've got the jackpot."

Something small and black hopped around the curve of the corridor behind him. Kin recalled that Marco, determinedly human, had been trying to make a pet of the raven. It was feeding time.

"I shall need assistance," Jalo said.

"You've got the self-filling purse," said Kin. "That sounds like a jackpot to me."

"Nah. With what's here we can start our own Company where we're going." He reached into a side pocket and pulled out a navigation reel. "It's all here."

"I would prefer to talk further without the piftol threatening uf," said Silver painfully. "It if not kind."

The raven flew up onto Jalo's shoulder and screamed in his ear—

—a stream of Clipe needles zonked into the ceiling—

—Marco moved so fast that his passage across the space separating him from Jalo could only be deduced from the fact that he was suddenly astride the fallen figure, the Clipe held in one hand and the other three raised to smash a skull—

—he blinked, and looked around as if waking from a dream.

He stared at Jalo, and then leaned forward.

"He's dead," he said helplessly. "I didn't even strike him."

Kin knelt down by the man.

"He was dead before you got there."

She had seen the face go snow-white after the bird's scream. Jalo had already been dropping when Marco reached him.

He was sufficiently recently dead for it to be worth slotting his body into the ship's medical sargo, which immediately flashed a row of red lights. Kin checked the readings on the panel below. Cell rupture, organ rupture, brain damage—when they got back to a human world it would be six months in a resurrection vat for Jalo.

"A coronary?" suggested Silver.

"Massive," said Kin. "He's lucky."

There was silence, and when Kin turned the shand was looking at her in astonishment.

"Coronary is easy," she explained. "We can repair that. Simple job. If Marco had got to work on him there wouldn't have been anything left to put in a vat. He *threatened* Marco."

Silver nodded. "Kung are paranoid. But he also acts like a human."

"You watch him enter a room. That walk of his is a fighting stance. Kung don't know the meaning of the word fear."

"Fine," said Silver pleasantly. "Half kung, half human. Well, I know the meaning of the word fear, and right now I'm scared."

"Yeah, I can see—"

(a few seconds of vertigo, an eternity of despair)

The first thing Kin registered when her sight came back was the cabin window and the view outside. The ship appeared to be surrounded by a fog full of icebergs.

She was dimly aware of an alarm, which cut off abruptly.

She was aware of hazy stars, and of drifting across the cabin because there was no gravity. Silver was floating near what had been the ceiling, out cold.

Let's see. The ship had been floating on a lake. Now it was floating in space. Outside was frozen air and quite a bit of the lake, so down on Kung storms must be raging, since a few cubic hectares of air and water had suddenly been dragged into space inside the ship's Elsewhere field. . . .

In free fall Kin's natural genius felt somewhat cramped. She swam and bounced her way to the control room, where Marco was hunched over the main consol like a spider, and screamed in his ear.

He grabbed her out of the air and turned her to face the big screen at the far side of the cabin.

She stared, open-mouthed.

After a while she fetched Silver, who was treating a slight headwound in the medical room and cursing in several languages, and made her watch.

When the film was finished they ran it through again.

"I put Jalo's reel in the navigator," said Marco finally. "It included this."

"Run it again," said Kin. "I want to have another look at one or two bits."

"The picture quality is exceptionally good," said Marco.

"It had to be. They were meant to be transmitted over tens of parsecs—"

"If I may interrupt for a few seconds," said Silver. She reached up to her tusks, and began to twist them. Kin watched in fascinated horror as the fangs unscrewed and were stowed away in a small leather case. She had seen fangless shand on Shand itself, but they were children or condemned criminals.

"In order to be a good linguist one must be prepared to make sacrifices," said Silver in faultless allspeak. "Do you think I submitted to the operation without much secret shame and soul-searching? However, I have something to say. Do I strike you, Marco Farfarer, as a character of ill humor and short temper?"

"No. Why?"

"If you try a stunt such as you just did once more, I will kill you."

"I thought it was impossible anyway," said Kin, with hasty diplomacy.

Marco looked from one to the other.

"It's not impossible, simply tricky and highly illegal," he said carefully. "Do it wrong, and you end up in the middle of the nearest sun. As for your, uh, statement, Silver—I have noted it."

They both nodded gravely.

"Right," said Kin brightly. "Fine. Now show the film again."

Either the film was genuine or Jalo was an unsung special-effects genius.

It might have been the polar regions of New Earth, or anywhere on Serendipity. Not Njal and Milkgaard, because those worlds had no birds and one picture showed a flock of birds in the distance—until Silver turned up the magnification. Whatever they were, they were not birds. Not with those horse heads, black scales and bat-black wings. But there was a word for them in human history, and the name "dragon" unfolded in Kin's mind.

There was a seascape, and unless there was something very wrong with the size of the waves, the snake-headed beast looping through them was fully a kilometer long.

There were distant views of what might have been cities. There were several sunsets, at least one taken from the air, and a number of night shots of starscapes.

"Go back to the aerial sunset," said Kin. "Now what's wrong?"

"Horizon's odd," said Marco.

It was. The curve was oddly flattened. There was something else wrong too, something Kin couldn't immediately spot.

"Apart from that, it could be any human world," observed Silver.

"Funny," said Kin. "Jalo talked about a flat Earth, not just a flat world."

"That does not surprise me. Humans have been the only race to entertain the primitive idea of a flat world," said Marco, running the film back to the starscapes. "If you don't believe me, look it up. Kung always thought they lived on the inside of a sphere, and shandi always had big Twin hanging up there to teach them a basic lesson in cosmology."

Kin grunted. Later on she found time to check it in the ship's library. It was true, but what did it prove? That men were slightly stupid and very egocentric? Aliens already knew that.

"We shall be able to ascertain the precise nature of the flat world," said Marco, "when we arrive."

"Hold it," said Kin. "Stop right there. What do you mean, when we arrive?"

The kung gave her a withering look. "I have already set up the program. That whine you hear is the matrix battery charging up."

"Where are we now?"

"Half a million kilometers from Kung."

"Then you can land and let me off. I ain't coming!"

"What plans had you, then?"

Kin hesitated. "Oh, we could take Jalo to a resurrection clinic," she said at last. "We could wait around and, uh, we, uh . . ."

She stopped. It sounded pretty feeble, even to her.

"We have the course, the ship and the time," said Marco. "The man will come to no harm in the sargo. If we hesitate we will have to explain, and probably the Company will want to know why you weren't frank with it in the first place."

Kin looked at Silver for support, but the shand just nodded heavily. "I would not like to lose this opportunity," she said.

"Look," said Kin. "Taking this trip with Jalo seemed a good idea, right? But now we don't know the half of what we're embarking on. I'm just using a bit of intelligent caution, is all."

"So much for the vaunted monkey curiosity," said Marco to Silver. "So much for the dynamic manifest destiny we hear so much—"

"You're mad—the pair of you!"

Marco shrugged, a particularly effective gesture with two sets of shoulders, and unfolded his bony frame from the pilot chair. "Okay," he said. "You fly us back."

Kin flumped into the seat and pulled the wraparound screen down to her level. She looked at the three-quarter consol. There were several dials that looked vaguely familiar. That black panel might control air and temperature; the rest was gibberish. Kin was used to ships with big brains.

"I can't fly this!" she said. "And you know it!"

"Glad to have you with us, then," said Marco, looking at his watch. "Why don't you two get some sleep?"

Kin lay in her bunk, thinking. She thought of how attitudes to aliens got stereotyped. Kung were paranoid, bloodthirsty and superstitious. Shandi were calm, bloodthirsty and sometimes ate people. Shandi and kung thought humans were bloodthirsty, foolhardy and proud. Everyone thought Ehfts were funny, and no one knew what Ehfts thought about anyone.

It *was* true that once four kung had boarded a grounded human ship during the bad old days and killed thirty-five crew before the last kung went down under the weight of Clipe needles. It *was* true that on certain diplomatically forgotten occasions shandi had, with great ceremony, eaten people. So what? How could you evaluate this unless you could think like an alien?

We dismiss each other with a few clichés, she thought. It's the only way we can live with one another. We have to think of aliens as humans in a different skin, even though we've all been hammered by different gravities on the anvils of strange worlds. . . .

She sat up in the darkness, listening. The ship hummed to itself.

She padded naked down the equatorial corridor. Something that had been nagging at the back of her mind had surfaced, and she had to find out. . . .

Ten minutes later she entered the control room, where Marco was still sitting under the screen.

"Marco?"

He ducked his head, then pushed the screen up and grinned.

"Everything's going fine. What's that you're holding? It looks like a melted plastic sculpture."

"This was the box the raven was in. Bioplastic. It doesn't melt below a thousand degrees. I found it in the airlock," snapped Kin, tossing it onto his lap.

Marco turned the shapeless mass over, then shrugged.

"Well? Are these birds intelligent?"

"Sure, but they don't tote cutting torches around."

There was a pause while they both gazed at the melted box.

"Jalo could have done it," said Marco uncertainly. "No, that doesn't work—he was surprised to see the bird."

"To put it mildly, yes. I don't like this sort of mystery, Marco. Have you seen the raven?"

"Not since Jalo did. Hmm." He reached out one lank arm and punched the ship's panic button.

Bells and sirens echoed through the ship. Within forty

seconds Silver thundered in, crushed snow from her sleeping pit still sticking to her fur. She braked when she saw them watching her, and growled.

"A human joke?" she said. They told her.

"It *is* odd," she agreed. "Shall we search the ship?"

Marco spoke at length about the number of small spaces in a spaceship. He added details about what happened if something small and feathered crawled into a vital duct, or blundered into the wrong cable.

"All right," said Kin. "What are you going to do?"

"You two go back to your rooms," said Marco. "Seal them off, and search for the bird. I will evacuate the rest of the ship. This is standard anti-vermin drill anyway."

"But you'd kill it," said Kin.

"I don't mind."

Later Marco sat watching the build-up of power in the ship's fusion driver, out there in the center of the toroid's ring field, and wondered about the bird. Then he dismissed the thought, and wondered instead if either of the others had noticed him hide the magic money purse after Jalo's death. Just a matter of prudence. . .

Silver turned over in the snow hole in her environmentally frozen cabin, and wondered if either of the others had seen her remove the magic purse from Marco's hideaway and secrete it in one of her own. For later evaluation. . .

Kin lay watching the blinking red light that indicated vacuum in the corridor outside her cabin, and felt a vague sympathy for the raven. Then she wondered if either of the others had seen her take the magic purse from the place Silver had hidden it and drop it out of a disposal shute during an Elsewhere jump. By now the purse was barreling on toward the edge of Universe, propelled by the steady ejection of Day bills from its open mouth.

Spaced at four arbitary compass points around the ship were quick-air chambers, installed during its construction to conform with Board of Trade regulations. They meant that if caught during sudden decompression a crewman could duck into a chamber instead of having to struggle with a suit. They were a good idea.

The big red light on each one was supposed to flash so that later rescuers could see it. There was no one to see it now, but one was flashing.

Inside, both claws gripping the pressurizing lever, the raven leaned with its beak pressed against the air vent, and thought about survival.

During a dull moment, of which any voyage had plenty, Silver once asked the ship's library to provide her with a copy of *Continuous Creation*. It couldn't, but it did furnish this extract from the relevant *Ten Worlds Literary Digest*—after 167 lines on the book's contribution toward the rediscovery of paper making.

"The book's achievement was that it drew together a few dozen strands of research on archaeological, paleontological and astronomical fronts, and wove the Theory out of them. It is easy now to say that, of course, the Theory was obvious. Obvious it was, but it was so obvious that it was almost hidden—except to a planetary designer who was used to thinking in terms of secondary creation, and who was also a voracious reader." This was the Theory:

There were the Spindles; telepaths, so telepathic that no more than a thousand of them could occupy a world at a time, because of the mental static. And we humans thought we had a population problem. They left libraries and scientific devices, and it was already known that they could reshape planets more to their liking. They needed room to think. They were proud. When they discovered, on Bery, the remains of a Wheeler strata machine under half a mile of granite, their pride was shattered. Spindles were not, as they had believed, the first lords of Creation—the Wheelers had beaten them to it, half a billion years before. The shock led them to cease reproduction.

One ship, conveniently stocked with library tapes, had eventually tumbled slowly enough across Earth's system to be stopped. Inside its meteor-ripped skins were three mummies. They had been the crew. Three crew.

The ship had been over a hundred miles across. Most of it had been empty balloon. Room to *think*. . .

The Wheelers were silicon hemispheres, propelling themselves on three natural wheels. Nothing except shell and wheels had survived, but there were, under the granite, the compressed remains of Wheeler cities. Other Wheeler remains began to be discovered.

Wheelers had recorded traces of an earlier race, the paleotechs. Paleotechs were said to have created the Type

II stars and their planets. One of their specialities had been the triggering of novas as a crucible for heavy-metal creation. Why? Why not? Paleotechs weren't easily understandable. (Once, Kin Arad answered to her own satisfaction at least the question of why the paleotechs had created stars. "Because they could," she said.)

In one interstellar gulf a ship dropping out of Elsewhere for repairs had discovered a paleotech—dead, at least by human terms (though Kin Arad has pointed out that paleotechs probably lived by a different time scale and that this apparently lifeless hulk may have been very much alive if considered by slow, metagalactic Time). It was a thin-walled tube half a million miles long.

Wheeler legends spoke of a polished smooth world where paleotechs had inscribed their history, which included the legend of the pre-paleotech ChThones, who spun giant stars out of galactic matter, and the RIME, who produced hydrogen as part of their biological processes. . . .

This was the Theory: that races arose, and changed the universe to suit themselves, and died. And then other races arose in the ruins, changed the universe to suit themselves, and died. And other races arose in the ruins—and arose, and arose, all the way back to the pre-Totalic nothingness. Continuously creating. There had never been any such thing as a *natural* universe.

(Kin once heard a speaker refer disparagingly to the Spindles because they had manipulated worlds. She stood up and said: "So what? If they hadn't, Earth would still be a mess of hot rocks and heavy clouds. They changed all this and they brought in a big moon, but do you know the best of all? They gave us a past. They jiggered their strata machines to give us fossils of things that had never existed. Icthyosaurs and crinoids and chalk and ancient seas. Maybe they didn't feel at home unless they had a few hundred meters of fossil strata under them, as they couldn't feel happy if there was another Spindle within fifty miles. But *I* think they did it because it was their art. They didn't know anyone would see it, but they went ahead and did it.")

Kin found a quiet moment to explore the weapons hold. If Marco had flown the ship to a world with a shaky government, there was enough stuff on board to equip a *rebel* army. There was what looked like a complete missile system, and several racks of small arms that Jalo must have had made to ancient patterns. One handgun *fired* sharp wooden bullets. Why?

The ship—they never did get round to naming it—dropped into real space. Marco's hands hovered over the controls as he waited for a welcoming barrage.

There was nothing. There wasn't even a star near the ship.

"We're still on the edge of explored space," said Marco. "That blue giant there is Dagda Secundus. It's about half a light-year away."

"Well, here we are and where are we?" said Kin. "A star like that shouldn't have planets, especially nice sunny ones."

"The computer is searching," said Marco gloomily. "Needle. Haystack. Perhaps we'll find some iceball whipping along at maybe twenty knots orbital velocity."

"Meanwhile, we could eat," suggested Silver.

They each dialed their meal from the dumbwaiter and wandered back into the control room.

"Give it an hour," said Kin. "This area of space has been explored. What the hell can it find that the survey teams missed?"

"I doubt if they looked out here," said Silver. There was a brief moment of nausea as the computer flicked the ship a few million miles for a parallax measurement.

"We followed Jalo's course tape," said Marco. "I'd hate to have to—"

The computer chimed. Marco vaulted into the control chair and juggled the screen controls.

At the limit of magnification there was a small fuzzy hemisphere. They looked at it blankly.

"Just a planet," said Kin.

"Rather brightly lit for this distance out," agreed Marco. "Highly polished ice?"

Silver coughed apologetically. "I am no astronomer," she said, "but surely it is wrong?"

"Not ice?" said Marco. "Could be Helium IV, I suppose."

"You misunderstand me," said the shand. "Surely the light hemisphere should be pointed *toward* the star?"

They stared at it. Finally Marco exclaimed, "Bleeding hell, she's right!" He glanced down at the shouter screens. "It's half a billion miles away," he said. "I should be able to make a straight-line jump. Uh. . ."

For a moment four hands hovered like a flight of hawks over the controls.

And dropped.

The sky was falling in on them. Then Marco, almost in hypnosis turned the ship and there, spread out below like a bowl of jewels, was the flat Earth.

It was like a plate full of continents. A coin tossed into the air by an indecisive god.

The ship had come out perhaps twenty thousand miles above it, and out of vertical. Kin looked out at a hazy map of black land and silver sea, fuzzed with moonlit cloud. There was what, for want of a better term—how many people had mapped flat planets?—a polar cap, hugging one side of the disc.

Moonlit? There was a moon, apparently a few thousand miles above the disc, and it *shone*. It couldn't be reflected light. There was nothing to reflect. And there were stars—between the ship and the disc, there were stars.

The shadowy oval lay inside a hazy globe. Marco translated what the machines were emotionlessly telling him. The disc was inside a transparent sphere sixteen thousand miles across, and the stars were—"that's what I said, Kin"—were fixed to this.

One edge of the disc glowed brighter. It flashed green fire, which ran around the rim until they were looking at a hole in space surrounded by green and silver flames. Then the ring grew a gem, and died as suddenly as it had come. The sun had risen. A tiny sun.

One machine said it was an external fusion reactor. It looked like a sun.

This is what I'll remember, thought Kin. The green fire at sunrise, because all around the disc there's a sea, and it flows over the edge in a waterfall thirty-five thousand miles long and the sun shines through the falling water—no wonder Jalo was mad.

Dawn rushed across the disc. Silver was the first to react. She giggled.

"He did call it a flat Earth, didn't he?" she asked. "It was the truth, wasn't it?"

Kin looked. The continents had moved, it was true, and there didn't appear to be a New World at all. It was Earth down there—she recognized Europe. Earth. And it was flat.

Marco put them into a fast orbit, and no one left the cabin for three hours. Even Silver let a mealtime go past, and fed on curiosity instead.

They watched the waterfall slide past under high magnification. There were rocky islands, some tree-lined, overhanging the drop. It was a long drop—five hundred miles into a turmoil of steam. But the disc itself was only five miles thick. As the ship passed under the disc there was nothing but a space-black plain on the underside.

"Some humans used to believe the world was flat and rested on the backs of four elephants," said Silver.

"Yeah?" said Kin. "What did the elephants stand on?"

"A giant turtle, swimming endlessly through space."

Kin tasted the idea. "Stupid," she said. "What did the turtle breathe?"

"Search me. It's *your* racial myth."

"I'd give a lot to know how the seas can keep on spilling over the edge."

"Probably a molecule sieve, down there in the stream," said Marco without looking up from the shouter screens. "The plumbing is a minor matter, however. Where are the inhabitants? This thing is obviously an artifact, a created thing."

"No one's trying to contact us?"

"Just listen to my excitement."

"I suppose you mean no. Perhaps it's as well. I keep thinking of all those weapons in the hold."

"The thought seldom leaves my mind. Perhaps Jalo meant to hunt sea serpents, but I think not. I cannot help thinking that anyone capable of building the artifact would hardly be bothered by any weaponry this ship could carry."

"Perhaps the inhabitants are dead," suggested Silver.

Kin and Marco looked at each other blankly.

"Unlikely," said Marco. "More likely they've passed beyond the stage of gross physical existence. Maybe even at this moment they are screwing the inscrutable."

"They're due for a big shock one of these days, then," said Kin. "This setup must take vast amounts of power just to keep it going. The sun's orbit is all wrong. What keeps the seas from emptying? Why have they got their own private stars when there's real ones out here—"

"I can answer that one," said Marco. "It looks as though

the big sphere is transparent only from the outside. We can see in, they can't see out. Don't ask me why."

"Do we land?" said Silver.

"How could we get in?" said Kin. Marco grimaced.

"That is easy," he said. "There's an eighty-meter hole in the shell. We passed it last orbit."

"What?"

"You were busy looking at the waterfall and in any case it did not seem particularly important. No doubt the disc-dwellers have space travel."

They hovered over the hole twenty minutes later. It was slightly elliptical, and the edges seemed to have been melted. It could have been made by careful jockeying of a ship with a fusion drive, thought Kin. Or a geological laser. Would a Terminus probe have carried one? Probably.

"We're still way above atmosphere," said Marco. "I hope the disc-dwellers aren't sore about people making holes in the sky."

"We could offer to pay for repairs," said Silver.

Kin wondered if that was a joke. Why would anyone shut themselves away from the universe like this? It didn't make sense, unless they were completely paranoid. If they weren't to start with they would be now.

"No," she said out loud. "They couldn't have built something like this if they were mad."

"It looks like Earth, and Earthmen are mad," Silver pointed out. "I suppose humans haven't been doing a little secret world building?"

"No . . ." began Kin, and saw they were both looking at her slyly. "I don't know," she finished lamely. "It certainly looks like it, I'll admit."

"It certainly does," said Marco.

"It does too," agreed Silver.

"Don't breathe," said Marco. "There's just enough room. We're going in."

The ship dropped through with a few meters to spare, and the proximity detectors shrilling. They were still going mad when Kin looked up and saw a ship speeding toward them.

It hit in one of the holds, buckling the hull and sending the sky wheeling crazily. Damage doors crashed into place and then the control room lurched again as it fell away from the ship under its own power, a self-contained emergency craft.

The damage to the ship was nothing to what happened to the attacker. It disintegrated.

Blue-green shards were spreading across the sky, and as Kin pulled herself up from the cabin floor, the screens were sparkling like glitter dust.

The inner door of the emergency airlock opened and Marco loped in, tugging his helmet with two hands. Another one held a laser rifle, salvage from the other half of the ship. The fourth held a long sliver of glass, gingerly.

"Looks like someone threw a bottle at us," said Kin.

"Their aim was remarkable," said Marco coldly. "I can take us back to the rest of the ship, but it is hardly worth it. We've got no Elsewhere capability. I can't build a pinch field. Most of the contents of the hold are floating out there somewhere, and they were our weapons. The auxiliary systems are all working. I could probably fly us home on the ringrim motor alone."

"Then all is not lost," rumbled Silver.

"No, except that it would take about two thousand years. Even this bloody gun is useless. Someone thought it a safe idea to pack the main coil in a separate box."

"So we land on the disc," said Kin flatly.

"I was wondering when someone was going to say that," said Marco. "It'll be a one-way trip. This craft won't lift off again."

"What hit us?" said Silver. "I thought I saw a ball about ten meters across. . . ."

"I've got a horrible feeling I know what it was," murmured Kin.

"Yes. It was a weapon," said Marco. "I admit I find its complete destruction difficult to understand, but the fact remains that we had a stargoing ship. Now we have not. I intend to make one orbit before landing."

Silver coughed gently. "What," she said, "will we eat?"

It took several hours to ferry the dumbwaiter across from the lazily spinning ship. At Kin's insistence they also brought the sargo with Jalo in it, and linked it into the emergency system. The waiter had its own internal power supply—as laid down by regulations. No one wanted to spend his last hours in a blacked-out ship with any hungry shandi that might be aboard.

The new orbit took them past the disc's moon, no longer

shining and obviously invisible in the disc's day sky. They saw that one hemisphere was black.

"Phases," said Kin. "Wobble the moon on its axis and you get phases."

"Who does the wobbling?" asked Marco.

"I don't know. Whoever wanted this thing to look like Earth, from the surface. And don't look at me like that—I'll swear this wasn't built by humans."

She spoke to them about artificial worlds—rings, discs, Dyson spheres and solar tunnels.

"They don't work," she said. "That is, they're vulnerable. Too dependent on civilization. And there's too many things to go wrong. Why do you think the Company terraforms worlds when there are cheaper alternatives? Because planets last, that's why. Through anything.

"And I'm certain this wasn't built by Spindles. Planets were *important* to them. They had to feel the strata below and the unlimited space above. Somehow they could sense it. Living on something like this could drive them out of their skulls. Anyway, they died out four million years ago at least, and I'm positive that this thing isn't that old. It must be all machinery just to keep going, and machines wear out."

"There's cities down there," said Marco, "in the right place, too. If this was Earth." He looked up. "Okay, Kin, you've been dying to tell us. What did hit us back there?"

"Was the hole on the ecliptic?"

Marco leaned over and played with the computer terminal for a few seconds. "Yes," he said, "Is it important? The sun was well below us."

"We were pretty unlucky. I think we were hit by a planet."

"That was my thought too," said Silver gravely, "but I did not like to say anything in case I was thought a fool."

"Planet?" asked Marco. "A planet landed on the ship?"

"I know it's usually the other way around, but I think I'm beginning to grasp the workings of this system," replied Kin. "There's a fake sky, so there's got to be fake planets. *Their* orbits must be something to see. If it's really supposed to look like an Earth sky they'd have to be retrograde sometimes."

"I was wrong," said Marco. "We should have started for home. We could have rigged up the sargo and taken turns to wake up. Two thousand years isn't all that long. I don't know what agency told Jalo I was the man for the job, but he's owed his money back."

"Still, the view's good," said Kin.

The ship was passing under the disc again. And again there was the flash of green fire as, for a few seconds, the sun shone through the waterfall around the disc.

Something hit them—again.

It wasn't a planet. It was a ship, and the most of it was still hanging in the rearward aerial array when Marco had fought the spin it gave them.

Kin went out this time, and she steadied herself on an aerial stump as she looked at the frosted wreckage.

"Marco?"

"I hear you."

"It's made one hell of a mess of the antennae."

"I have already deduced that. We are also losing air. Can you see the leak?"

"There's fog damn near everywhere. I'm going to take a look."

They heard her boots clump around the hull, and then there was a silence so long that Marco shouted into the radio. When Kin spoke, she spoke slowly.

"It is a ship, Marco. No, wrong word. A boat. A sailing boat. You know, like on seas."

She looked across at the fire-rimmed disc.

A waterfall pouring over the edge of the world.

The mast was broken and most of the planking had been whirled away by the force of the impact, but enough rope had held together to make it obvious the boat had a passenger.

"Marco?"

"Kin?"

"It had a passenger."

"Humanoid?"

Kin growled. "Look, it went over the waterfall and then into vacuum and then hit the ship! What sort of description do you want? It looks like an explosion of a morgue!"

Kin was used to violent death. Oldsters died that way—freefall diving without a backpack on, deliberately wandering near when they released the cloned elephants on a new world, banjaxing the safeties and stepping into the hopper of a strata machine—but then ambulance crews took over.

There had never been anything to see, except in the strata machine case. And that was only a strange pattern in a freshly laid coal measure.

She knelt like a robot. Wet cloth had frozen in vacuum, but it had been good cloth, well woven. Inside . . .

Silver later analyzed tissue samples, and announced that the passenger had been human enough to call Kin cousin. She would have been surprised at any other result, without being able to say quite why.

He had sailed over the edge of the world. The thought made her go cold. Everyone knew the world was flat, everyone had always known the world was flat: It was obvious. But there was always someone who would laugh at the old men and voyage into the terrifying seas to prove a different theory. And he had been horribly wrong.

Kin was glad about the argument over the suits. There were five, two of which were shand size. One of the others seemed to be faulty, and the trio were all sufficiently space-cautious not to trust a suspect suit.

"We must take the dumbwaiter," said Silver. "Maybe you and Kin will be able to eat what is down there, but I will be poisoned."

"Get the machine to dish out a sack of dried food concentrates then," ordered Marco. "We need that fourth suit."

Silver grunted. "Not as much as we need the machine. It can analyze food. It can supply clothing. If necessary we can live off it."

"I'm inclined to agree," said Kin.

"It'll take the lifting power of the entire suit!"

"Would you rather take a laser rifle that won't fire?" said Silver. They glared at each other.

"Let's take it for Silver's sake," said Kin hurriedly. "Hunger can be a big problem for shandi."

Marco shrugged twice. "Take it then," he said, and snatched the tool kit from a wall locker. While they manhandled the big machine into the space suit and padded it around with thermoblankets, he took the control chair apart and ended up with a strip of metal trim sharpened to a killing edge and with a plastic handle at one end. Kin watched him weigh it thoughtfully in his hand. Ready to take on the makers of a fifteen-thousand-mile-wide world with a homemade sword. Was that commendable human spirit or stupid kung bravado?

He turned and saw her watching him.

"This is not to put fear into them," he said, "but to take fear out of me. Are we ready?"

He programmed the autopilot to hover for ten minutes a few hundred miles from the waterfall. They took off on the suits' lift belts. Silver towing the spare suit on a length of monofilament Line.

Kin glanced over her shoulder as the ship sped away on a spear of flame and climbed toward a high orbit. Then she turned back to the great wall of water, and the little islands on the very edge. Way around the disc the orbiting sun was sinking.

There were no city lights, anywhere.

In a ragged line they flew toward the tumbling water and the thunder at the edge of the world.

No one had seen, just before the ship soared away, the now perfectly workable fifth suit tumble from the airlock. It inflated instantly, like an empty balloon.

In the big bubble helmet the raven surveyed the emergency controls carefully. The suits were designed for anything—they could fly across a star system and land on a world. There were tongue controls.

The raven reached out, pecked gently. The suit surged forward. The raven watched intently, then tried another control. . . .

The dawn came wetly. Kin awoke soaked with dew. So much for thermoblankets.

It had been a long night. The island, at the very lip of the rimfall was hardly big enough to support a dangerous carnivore, unless it was semiaquatic. But Marco had pointed out that the disc might abound with semiaquatic carnivores, and had insisted on mounting guard. Kung could do without sleep for weeks at a time.

Kin wondered whether to tell him about her personal stunner, now carefully hidden in a suit pocket. Feeling like a heel, she decided not to. She had a long struggle with her conscience but she won, she won.

Marco had evidently slept with the coming of the sun. He lay curled bonelessly under a dripping bush. Through the mists, Kin saw Silver sitting on the rock outcrop on the fall side of the island.

Kin scrambled up toward her. The shand grinned and made room for her on the sun-warmed stone.

The view was as though from the point of a wedge. The rocky peak rose out of what looked suspiciously like a small wood of ash and maple. Beyond, the sun glinted off silver-green sea. To either side the fall was a white line of foam seen dimly through mist clouds. Behind . . .

Silver grabbed her in time.

When Kin regained her balance she moved carefully down the slope to a seat that did not hang so obviously over a drop, and asked, "Can you really sit there and not worry?"

"What's to worry? You did not fret in the ship when there was only a meter of hull between you and eternity," said the shand.

"That's different. That's a *real* drop behind you."

Silver raised her muzzle and sniffed the air.

"Ice," she exclaimed. "I smell ice. Kin, may I give you a lecture on sunshine?"

Kin automatically squinted at the sun. Her memory told her it was asteroid-size. But it looked right for Earth. It felt right on her skin.

"Go ahead. Tell me something I don't know."

"I have noticed pack ice going over the fall. Why should this be? We know the disc has polar islands. Yet there are green lands nearby. Consider the distance between the equator and the polar islands. Why are not the north and south extremities frozen solid and the equatorial regions burning?"

Kin leaned her chin on her hands. The shand was talking about the inverse square law. If the sun was eight thousand miles from the equator at noon, it was eleven thousand miles from what had to be called the poles.

Well, the path that sun followed couldn't be called an orbit. It moved like a guided spaceship. But that didn't explain the warm air around her. Consider: On most worlds the poles were but a few thousand miles farther from the primary than was the equator, yet the temperature was wildly different. On the disc, if one thought of the temperate zone as being effectively Earth-distant from the sun, then the poles were out around Wotan and the equator broiled like Venus.

"Some sort of force lens?" she hazarded. "I could believe

anything. Certainly the sun's path must be changed regularly."

"I do not understand."

"To get seasons."

"Ah . . . seasons. Yes, humans would require seasons."

"Silver—"

The shand sniffed again. "This is good air," she said.

"Silver, stop dodging. Yu think *we* built this."

"Ah—the kung and I have discussed the topic, it is true."

"The hell you have! We'd better get this clear. Humans may be mad, but we're not stupid. As a work of celestial mechanics this disc is about as efficient as a rubber wrench. It must drink power to keep going. For crying out loud, you don't want to hang your descendants' lives on the efficiency of dinky little orbiting suns and fake stars! Why didn't the disc builders orbit it around a real sun? They must have had the power. Instead they came out here to nowhere and built a world according to the ideas of some kind of medieval monk. That's not human."

"The man on the ship was human."

Kin had been thinking hard and long about him. Sometimes he came into her thoughts unbidden, in the long sleep hours. She hesitated before replying.

"I . . . don't know. Maybe the disc builders kidnapped a bunch of humans back in prehistory. Or perhaps there was parallel evolution somewhere. . . ."

She felt angry at herself for her ignorance, and even angrier at the shand for diplomatically not picking at the big holes in her argument. If someone had offered Kin an instant return to the comforts of Earth at that moment, she would have spat. There were too many questions to be answered first.

Out loud: "Jalo talked about matter transmission. I wonder how they get the water up from the bottom of the fall back into the ocean?"

Marco scrambled up the rocks toward them. A change had come over him since the landing on the disc. On the ship Kin remembered him as being moody, cynical—now he seemed to vibrate with undirected enthusiasm.

"We must make plans," he said.

"You have a plan," Kin corrected.

"It is imperative we contact the masters of the disc," said Marco, nodding and not appearing to notice her sarcasm.

"You have changed your mind, then." Silver's voice floated down from the heights. She was standing up, sniffing the air again.

"I face facts, however distasteful. We cannot repair the ship. They will have the capacity to do so, or spacecraft we may hire. Jalo got back. Or do you wish to spend your life here?"

"I do not think the disc people can help us," said Silver. "We detected no power sources, no energy transmission. We landed unaccosted. These are my secondary reasons for suspecting a lapse into barbarianism."

"Secondary?" said Kin.

Silver grunted. "There is a ship approaching," she said. "By its lines I do not suspect it is a sports plaything of an advanced race."

They stared at her, then raced up the crag. Marco beat Kin to the top by a series of long leaps and peered out across the water.

"Where? Where?"

Kin saw a speck on the edge of sight.

"It is a rowing ship, twelve oars to a side," said Silver, squinting slightly. "There is a mast and a furled sail. It stinks. The crew stink. On their present course they will pass a mile to the north."

"Over the falls?" said Kin.

"Surely the disc people have mastered the art of dealing with the waterfall," said Marco. "The current does not appear to be strong. There is a weir effect."

Kin thought of the man in the fallen boat.

"They know they're heading for the falls but they don't know what the falls are," she said. Silver nodded.

"They stink because they are afraid," she said. "They are changing course for this island. There is a man standing in the forward end, looking toward the falls."

Marco became a blur of action.

"We must prepare," he hissed. "Follow me down." Rocks crashed behind him as he bounded back toward the trees where they had spent the night.

Kin glanced from the shand, standing like a statue, to the boat. Even she could see the figures now. Water gleamed as it cascaded off whirling oars. She even thought she could hear shouts.

"I don't think they will make it," she said quietly.

"That is so," said Silver. "See how the current swings them around."

'It may be a test," said Kin. "I mean, the very day we're here and all."

Silver sniffed. "My nose says not."

They looked at each other. Kin certainly was not going to argue with 350 million smell cells. She could see the men in the boat clearly. There was one, a small, bearded man, racing between the bent rowers and urging them on. At best the boat was standing still.

"Ahem," suggested Silver.

Kin squinted up at the sun.

"You recall that Line we're using to tow the spare suit?" she said. "How long is it?"

"Standard monofilament length, fifteen hundred meters," said Silver, adding, "It could tether a world."

"Of course, we could be making a big mistake," said Kin, starting to run down the slope. Silver lumbered after her.

"The stomach says not," she said. Kin smiled. Shandi had different ideas about the seat of the emotions.

She flew out in a suit lift belt shorn of the bubble suit, dragging one end of the cable by a wide loop.

"I consider this foolhardy in the extreme," said Marco's voice in her earpiece.

"Maybe," said Kin. "Just remember it was me that went out to the crashed boat."

There was a pause, with just the hissing of the wind in one ear and the carrier wave in the other. Finally Marco said, "Point your belt camera at the boat."

The rowers had seen her. Most of them were hanging transfixed on their oars.

The boat was perhaps twenty-five meters long, built like a pod. Silver had been too critical. Whoever had built it had a keen knowledge of hydrodynamics. There was one mast, amidships, with a furled sail. What space there was among the rowers appeared to be filled with jars and bundles.

Kin aimed at the red-haired man in the prow and dived, skimmed the wavetops and braked on a level with his astonished face, dropping the cable loop over the ornate prow and yelling to Silver. Spray drenched her as the cable sprang out of the water.

"Get them rowing," said Kin, making desperate arm movements. "To the island," she insisted, pointing dramatically.

Redhair stared at her, at the island, at the taut cable and the curving wake of the ship as Silver took the strain. Then he vaulted down the length of the boat, screaming at the bewildered men. One stood up and started to argue. Redhair picked up a spar from the deck and hit him hard, then hauled him from his place and took his oar.

Kin barreled skyward, looking down on a ship that was already leaving a wake like a powerboat. Then she leveled out and headed back to the island.

Its wooded shores passed far below her and she began searching in the misty blue sky beyond the falls.

She found what she was looking for. There was a tiny white speck, drifting outward. She swooped, hearing the slight *whump* as the belt's field took up a new protective shape around her.

Silver's belt motor was whining. Suit belts could lift their owner's against ten gravities, and Silver probably weighed five hundred pounds. It added up to a lot of pulling power at the end of the cable.

As Kin waved and turned back for the disc, Silver's voice grunted in her ear. "There have been several jerks on the cable."

Kin looked down. There was a swathe of felled timber across the island. The tree they'd used as an anchor hadn't been tough enough after all. Now the cable was bent around the crag itself.

"Everything's fine," she said. "We've got the edge on the current. The cable cut through some trees, that's all."

The boat was broadside on to the falls, but bouncing across the already whitening water.

"Fine, Silver," she said. "Fine. Marco wanted to meet the natives and he's going to get a basinful in a minute. Steady. Steady. Stop. *Stop!*"

The boat crunched on to the beach and bounded up into the trees, oars snapping. Several men fell overboard.

"We've beached it!" said Kin, dropping toward the wood.

"If they've got any imagination they're kissing that ground," said Silver.

"Right. Let's hope Marco has the sense to stay out of sight."

Her earpiece crackled. "I heard that. I wish to disassociate myself from this entire undertaking. . . ."

Kin swooped. She remembered being told that, ultimately, and whatever the science-fiction blats may say, no one ever learned a language by eavesdropping on a culture's communications.

It always came down to face-to-face confrontations. To pointing. To drawing circles in the sand.

Circles in the sand?

Well—it came down to pointing.

Much later she found Silver and Marco in their clearing higher up the slope. Silver was sitting beside the dumbwaiter, scooping handfuls of gray-and-red goo out of a bowl. Marco was lying full-length, peering through the leaves at the men on the beach.

They had lit a fire, and were cooking something.

Silver nodded at her and did something to the dumbwaiter's controls.

"I already ate," sighed Kin. "Some sort of grain meal and dried fish. Didn't you see?"

"I was, in fact, programming for an emetic."

Marco turned over. "You ate food without even a rudimentary analysis! Do you wish to die so soon?"

"We need their trust," said Kin. She tossed a sliver of fish to Silver. "I'll take your damn potion, but hold that under the 'waiter's nose. You know 'waiter food always tastes like somebody already ate it. While we're here we might as well have full stomachs."

She took a bowl of pink fluid from Silver's paw and retired to the other side of the clearing, where she was briefly and noisily sick. Silver reached up and dialed the waiter for coffee.

Presently the machine extruded a tongue of green plastic. She tore it out and read it.

"High on usable protein and vitamins," she said. "There is a hydrocarbon content from the dying process which may be carcinogenic in the long term, but it appears to pose no great risk."

"Great," said Kin, helping herself to coffee. "Suddenly I feel I could never look another dried fish in the face. Now, are you ready for the big answers? As far as I can understand it, the small red-haired man calls himself Leiv Eiriksson."

Silver flicked the green printout neatly into the machine's intake hopper.

"That is a remarkable coincidence or something else," she said calmly.

"You're not kidding."

Marco turned back from his surveillance. "What is coincidental?" he said. "Did you observe their weaponry?"

"They have swords made out of, uh, bog iron, hand-beaten. Easily blunted," said Kin thoughtfully. "Their greatest weapon is their boat. Are you familiar with the term 'clinker-built'?"

He nodded.

"Good; it means nothing to me. They're *fast*. These people rule a large part of the sea with those boats and those swords. Sometimes they are pirates, but they've got a sophisticated system of law. They're brave. A thousand-mile journey in a boat like that is commonplace."

Marco stared at her. "You learned all that?"

"No, all I understood was his name, and only because I've heard it before. It's all from memory." She looked at Silver for confirmation. The shand nodded.

" 'In the year three hundred and twenty-two,' " she intoned, " 'Eiriksson sailed the ocean blue.' "

"Very poetic," said Marco levelly. "Now, will you please *explain*?"

"If you were raised in Mexico you wouldn't have heard about this," said Kin. "They're snobbish about their history down there. Leiv Eiriksson . . ." She began to outline Earth's history. ". . . discovered Vinland, more than three hundred years after the Battle of Haelcor had ended the third and last Remen Empire."

The big migration followed automatically. The Turks were again pushing west and north. Leiv's father, Eirik, was a shrewd salesman. His Greenland had turned out nowhere like as green as it had been in his imagination, but from Vinland Leiv had thoughtfully brought rich berries and wild grains. The Northmen went west again.

They leapfrogged colony after colony down the eastern seaboard, up into the base rugged lands around Tyker's Sea and down the Long Fjord into the Middle Seas. It was the landscape of their dreams. They called it Valhalla.

There were natives. But the newcomers were only half-hearted farmers—underneath the agricultural veneer they thought bloody. Those tribes they couldn't outfight they outthought. When they met the Objibwa Confederacy they made treaties. And they spread, and merged.

By all the theories it should have ended there. Neither the natives nor the invaders had the textbook kind of social dynamic that builds Remes. The Northmen should have become just another tribe, with blue eyes and fair hair.

The theories were wrong. Something latent in both races was sparked into fire. It was a big continent, and it was rich.

In short, three hundred years after Leiv, a fleet arrived at the mouth of the Mediterranean. Most of the vessels were under sail, although there were one or two, small, fast and inclined to blow up, that could move into the wind. The sails of the big ships bore the Great Eagle of Valhalla on a striped background alternating the colors of the sky, the snow and blood.

The Battle of Gibraltar was short. Europe had been through two hundred years of stagnation.

There was no answer to cannon.

"I take the point," said Marco. "This Leiv is an important figure in Earth history. This is not, however, Earth."

"It looks like Earth," said Kin. "An Earth that was only imagined, but Earth."

"Are you seriously suggesting—"

"I'll tell you what I'm suggesting. I think you and Silver are right. I think humans built this place. I can't think why."

Silver grunted. "Surely there would be records—"

"Not if the Company suppressed them!"

It was the logical answer. The Company had built this artifact in secret. "Jalo" had been a plant, sent to bring them here. Why would the Company build the disc? Kin thought she knew the answer, and she didn't like it. But she couldn't figure out why there had been such a performance to bring them here.

But at least it was all logical. What other answer was there? Mysterious aliens? They would have to be very mysterious. If it was the Company, Kin hated it.

"We are in danger from every quarter," said Marco enthusiastically. "We must wear our lift belts at all times.

I suggest we move toward a center of civilization. We might find some clues as to the disc's origins."

"Then there's our transport," said Kin, pointing. "I don't know how long suit power lasts against gravity, but if there's any sea to cross I'd like to do it in a boat."

"They may yet turn out to be hostile," said Marco, watching the men.

"When they see you and Silver?"

In fact introducing the aliens presented a problem. Kin solved it by walking down to the encampment naked. After her earlier appearance as the goddess of mercy, she was confident that the men would sooner rape an alligator.

Leiv rushed toward her and sank to his knees. She looked down at him with an expression she hoped was benevolent.

He was smaller than most of the crew. She wondered how he exerted his authority—until she saw the shrewd glint in his eye, even now, that said here was the master of the unsporting kick and the kidney punch. She felt glad of the stunner, now concealed in her palm.

"You're about to have an amazing opportunity to make new friends," she said sweetly. "This is one saga they'll never believe. Okay, Silver, come on out."

The shand appeared at the decent distance, pushing through the bushes farther along the beach. As she plodded nearer several men hurried off in the other direction. When they saw her tusks several others followed them.

Grinning fit to burst, Kin walked across to the shand and put a hand in one huge, leather-palmed paw.

"Stop smiling," she said through clenched teeth.

"I fought it would put them at eafe?"

"On you it looks hungry."

Leiv was still standing rooted to the sand as Kin led the shand up to him. She took the man's hand in hers.

"Kneel and grovel," she murmured.

Silver folded up obediently. Leiv looked at her and then at Kin. Finally he reached out and prodded Silver's arm.

"Good boy," said Kin, beaming. He jumped back.

To introduce phase two Kin began to whistle the old robot-Morris tune *Mrs. Widgery's Lodger*.

Silver danced mournfully on the sand, gazing heavenward with an expression of acute distaste. But she held the rhythm. She also moved awkwardly. Kin, who had seen her move like oiled water, admired that last touch. Anything sufficiently ungainly was funny. Funny wasn't dangerous.

The men began to trickle back. Silver danced on, kicking up little sandstorms and shuffling from one foot to the other. Kin stopped whistling.

"You've passed," she said. "They're practically about to feed you lumps of sugar. Have a rest. Try to avoid yawning. Marco?"

Marco hissed. He stepped out of the bushes.

In his gray ship suit and a cloak hastily made out of a thermoblanket he looked passably human, if emaciated. His eyes were too big and his nose was too long. His face was gray as the suit.

But he had masses of flame-red hair. It wasn't really hair but it *was* red. Perhaps it made up for the eyes.

The men watched him warily, but no one fled this time.

One of them stepped up to Leiv and growled something, drawing a short sword. That led to a moment of confusion that ended with Marco crouched to spring and the man lying on the sand with his sword ten feet away. Then Leiv stopped twisting his arm and took a running kick. The man screamed.

"Now we launch the boat," said Kin firmly.

Silver padded toward the beached vessel and braced herself with a shoulder against the prow. Nothing happened for a moment, and then the boat slid down the beach, only stopping when the stern was moving urgently in the current.

Kin took Leiv's arm and led him firmly toward it. He was quick on the uptake. Within five minutes the men were on board, the dumbwaiter was humming to itself by the mast, and all eyes were on Silver, hovering out to sea on the end of the cable.

There was an area of dead water where the sea parted around the island before dropping into nothingness. By the time the current tugged feebly at it the boat was flying over the waves.

Two incidents enlivened the journey. Marco was handed a horn of some sweet substance by a nervous Leiv.

He sniffed it suspiciously and poured into the 'waiter. "It appears to be some kind of glucose drink," he said. "What do you think, Kin?"

"Did you try it on the 'waiter?"

"It gave a green light. Could it be some form of strengthening potion?"

He drank half the horn, and smacked what passed for lips. Then he laughed vaguely and drank the other half.

Later he programmed the dumbwaiter to duplicate it, and when the men had got over their amazement at the disposable plastic cups they were passed back as fast as they could be filled. Spasmodic singing broke out, and there was an occasional clattering of oars as rowers missed their stroke. Finally Kin, after Leiv's unspoken plea, switched off the machine.

Later Silver tried her hand at rowing. Sitting amidships and grasping two oars, she followed the stroke easily. One by one the rowers stopped to watch her. The boat didn't slow until her oars snapped.

Marco found Kin sitting in the skin shelter behind the mast, drinking martinis and thinking.

"I wish a private word," he said.

"Fine," said Kin, patting the rug beside her. "How is the head now?"

"Better. That drink obviously contains dangerous impurities. I don't think I will try any more for an hour or so." He fished in his belt pouch and pulled out a roll of plastic. It opened out into an aerial photograph of the disc.

"I got the computer to prepare it before we left the ship." he said.

"Why didn't you show it to me before?"

"I did not wish to encourage any foolhardy explorations. However, now that we are penetrating the disc . . . Look at the photo. What is missing?"

Kin took the sheet. "A lot," she said. "You know that. No Valhalla. That's why Leiv found the waterfall. No Brazil. The Peaceful Ocean is tiny, look, around here on the back of Asia—"

"Any additions?"

Kin peered at the map. "I don't know," she said. Marco used a double-jointed thumb to point to the center of the disc.

"The cloud cover makes it a bit indistinct, but *that* shouldn't be there. That island in the Arabian Sea. You notice it's perfectly circular? It is the geographical hub of the disc."

"What about it?"

"Don't you see? It is an anomaly. We'll find the disc civilization there if anywhere. These people are barbarians. Intelligent, yes—but spacegoing?"

He looked at her.

"Are you afraid this may turn out to be a Company artifact?" he said carefully. She nodded.

"There is an old kung story," said Marco softly, his voice like the currents in a quicksand, "concerning a lord who had a high tower built. Then he called various wise kung together and said, 'I will give my finest oyster farm and the famed kelp beds of Tchp-pch to the kung who can determine the height of that tower using nothing but a barometer. Those who fail will be exiled to the dry lands because that's the way it goes for the not-wise-enough.' So the wise kung tried and, although they could find the height to within a few *chetds*, this was not considered accurate enough and they were sent to the dry lands."

"I like folk tales," said Kin, "but do you think this is—"

"Then one day," said Marco loudly, "the wisest kung, who hadn't hazarded an answer yet, took his barometer to the home of the lord's master builder, and said, 'I will give you this beautiful barometer if you will be so good as to tell me the height of the tower.' "

A shadow loomed over them as Silver thrust her fangs over the deck awning.

"Forry to interrupt," she said, "but you might be interefted in thif. . . ."

They looked past her. Most of the men had stopped rowing and were staring up into the sky.

Kin stared with them. There were three specks moving across the haze like high-altitude jets.

"Vapor trails," said Marco. "Obviously They have come looking for us. We won't have to go and offer them our barometer."

"What can you see, Silver?" Kin asked. The shand twanged a fang.

"They appear to be flying lizards," she said. "The method of propulsion seems mysterious, but we may learn more, since they are losing height fast."

Leiv tugged at Kin's arm. Around them men were methodically tossing oars and bundles into the water and diving over the side after them. The little man seemed to be desperately searching for words. Finally he remembered one.

"Fire?" he suggested, and tumbled her backward into the sea. The coldness numbed her, but she knew enough to twist and kick out convulsively. Treading water and gripping a handy oar, she watched the sky. The specks had made a wide turn and the distant double thump of a sonic boom rolled across the sea. Marco and Silver had stayed on the boat, staring.

Soon three lizard-shapes with theatrically batlike wings glided over the wave tops to circle the boat in perfect formation, treading the air with two sets of cruel talons. Wisps of smoke trailed from their dilated nostrils.

Then they drifted off toward the north, becoming specks again as they made another turn. They also gained height. If they were aircraft, thought Kin, I'd say this was going to be a bombing run.

As the first dragon plummeted toward the ship, Leiv put one hand firmly on her head and pushed her underwater.

She bobbed up furious, her ears ringing. The water was steaming. Smoke was rising from the boat.

There was a sudden mound in the water beside her, and Marco surfaced, gasping and cursing. A bigger splash farther along marked Silver's return from the depths.

"What happened? What happened?" gasped Kin.

"It hovered and breathed fire," said Silver.

"And no bloody lizard does that to me!" screamed Marco. He struck out for the charred hull, rocking it violently in his attempt to get aboard.

Another beast drifted down. There was a quiet splash as Silver somersaulted and kicked away for the green depths.

There was also a groan from the water-treading men as they saw Marco uncloaked for the first time, grasping an oar with all four hands. As the dragon homed in it was bright enough to tread air just out of reach of Marco's impromptu weapon, wingbeats making spray patterns on the sea while it gathered its breath.

Something white shot through the water like a cork and gripped a pair of hovering claws. For a second Silver and the startled creature hung there. Then the wings met with a clap as they shot down into the sea, and Kin heard a distinct hiss.

The third dragon must have been the brightest, thought

Kin. The brightest *always* fought last. It was too late for it to stop its flight. Instead it passed over the boat with its wings spread like parachutes, and as it thundered by above his head, Marco screamed and leaped.

He was wearing his lift belt. The dragon tried to twist in midair, tumbled, regained its balance and tried to flee for height and safety. It didn't work.

On the other side of the boat the water foamed and a wingtip beat the surface listlessly. Then the hull canted sharply. Silver was climbing aboard.

The men around Kin shouted and struck out, laughing as they heaved themselves up the side.

High above the dogfight the surviving dragon screamed and disappeared speedily into the east, giving Kin a short and tantalizing glimpse of its high-speed propulsion. Those horror-story wings were too clumsy for anything except ponderous flight. To travel fast, the dragon folded them along its side, bent its head back under its body, and exhaled. By the time it was too far away for Kin to see details its breath was yellow-hot.

She followed something else down the sky as it tumbled lazily. It was a dragon head. Shortly afterward, although to the silent crowd on the boat it seemed much longer, the body followed, wings still spread wide, spiraling slowly with Marco climbing to its back and still hacking with the knife. When he hit the water a cheer went up.

It turned to anger when they saw that Silver was dragging her dragon aboard, still alive. When the men moved hurriedly aside they gave Kin a good view.

The beast flopped mournfully on the deck, water streaming from its wings. It raised its dripping head toward her and sneezed, violently.

Two jets of warm salt water hit Kin on the legs.

Marco was helped aboard by all four arms. His comb blazed blood-red and, as he stood up amid the admiring crowd, he raised his black-stained knife over his head and yodelled:

"Refteg! Ymal refteg PELC!"

Kin looked across at Silver, who was unscrewing her fangs. The shand grimaced.

"Tell me again about his being officially human," she said. "I keep forgetting."

"What," asked Kin, "do you intend doing with *that*?" One

of the men beside her had drawn his sword and was offering it proudly to the shand, hilt first. Silver ignored him.

"It's dead," she said, "but we have the body. I would very much like to know how an organic creature can breathe fire." She grabbed the corpse by neck and tail and dragged it aft.

Marco swaggered over to Kin.

"I triumph!" he shouted.

"Yes, Marco."

"They declare war on us! They sent dragons! But They reckoned without me!"

"Yes, Marco."

"Together They conspire against me yet I overcome!" he screamed, eyes glazed. Then his expression faded.

"You just think I'm a paranoid kung, don't you," he said sulkily.

"Since you mention it . . ."

"I'm proud to be human. Make no mistake! As for the other," he said, turning, "just because you're paranoid doesn't mean They aren't out to get you."

She watched him stride back to the men, who clustered around him. Frightened of everything except immediate physical danger. And as human as a tiger.

Silver was gazing ruefully at the dumbwaiter. It was not damaged, but the plastic paneling would never be the same again.

When the men were at the oars again Kin took out her suit, tool kit and arranged the dragon corpse as best she could on the tiny foredeck. The kit was small but comprehensive. A marooned spaceman could use it to survive on an alien world for years. Some had. Kin selected a medical scalpel.

Later she opened the kit fully and found a multi-chisel.

A minute later she reached in and assembled the vibrosaw. The *screeee* as it skidded and juddered over scales set her teeth on edge, but she didn't switch off until the blade broke.

She went to find Marco and Silver, who were taking a turn at the oars, and hunkered down between them.

"Those dragons are jet-powered," she said. "I could open the neck—it's lined with some sort of light spongy substance. It cut like jelly. When I tried the welding laser on it it didn't even warm up."

"How about the body?" said Marco.

"Those scales are *tough.* You will note I am holding the remains of a vibro-saw. They say a saw like this will cut hull metal."

Silver grinned. "One finds oneself thinking in terms of creatures that drink kerosene."

The kung snorted. "No doubt you neglected to run a geiger over it?" he said.

"No. I tested it all right. Nothing."

"I am surprised."

"Want to hear what happened when I cut the neck off and dropped the geiger head into the body cavity?"

"I am agog."

"It's as hot as hell in there. That creature is a living atomic furnace. And you can't tell me it evolved, not on an Earth-type world. It's a construct! That's where you'll find the disc builders—wherever that thing came from."

"The center of the disc," said Silver thoughtfully. Kin gawped, and the shand nodded casually as she leaned on the oar.

"I have some facility with languages, as you know," she said. "I have been talking to some of these men. We've got to the say-and-point stage. They see these things sometimes. In these parts they come from the east, but when the boats sail down south the dragons pass over from the northeast. Therefore I deduce they come from the central regions. Why are you staring?"

"Marco already wants to go to the center," said Kin. "He wants to offer them a barometer—I think."

The next dawn saw them sailing through an increasingly choppy sea into a fjord between white mountains. There was a colony of turf-roofed stone huts, and some sparse meadows. People hurried down to the shingle, then shied back noisily as, with the crew in their seats smirking like demons, Silver dropped over the side and ran the boat up the beach by herself.

There was a glassy-eyed dragon head roped to the prow.

Leiv led them into a long high-roofed hut that made Kin wonder whatever happened to Grendel. But of course, Grendel was slinking alongside her, swinging his too-many arms and eyeing the crowds for possible assassins.

When her eyes grew accustomed to the gloom inside she

saw an open fire in a pit and, beside it, a man sitting on a rough stool. One leg was stretched out in front of him. He was redheaded, and bearded.

He rose unsteadily from his stool and embraced Leiv, both men holding themselves as if there was just the faintest possibility that the other might attempt a stabbing. Then the younger man spoke.

It was a lengthy saga. After a while the older man was taken outside and shown what remained of the dead dragon. He was introduced to Silver, and hobbled several times around Marco, who looked at him sidelong. He grinned at Kin in a way that expressed horizontal desires.

Encouraged by this display, other inhabitants turned up. Kin's attention was drawn to two men in black robes. One of them was looking at Marco fearfully and reciting some sort of incantation.

Silver's head swiveled around.

She spoke a sentence in the same language.

From then on Silver did the translating.

"The tongue is Latin, the Remen tongue. Except that these men refer to Rome not Reme."

Kin considered it. "Romulus and Remus," she said at last. "The founders of Reme. Ever hear the legend?"

"I think I recall it in a folklore anthology."

"So on the disc Remus won the naming privilege. What else did they say?"

"Oh, quite a lot of gibberish about demons, the usual primitive-world stuff. Ever heard the word *troll*? They keep looking at Marco and saying it. There's also a lot about gods, I think."

Kin looked around. These people were either primitive or superb actors. Perhaps the gods were the disc builders.

"Ask about them," she said. A long conversation followed. Sometimes the older of the men would point to the sky. Leiv and his father watched carefully.

Finally Silver nodded and turned to Kin. "Let's see if I've got this right, now," she said. "There's a whole lot of gods about, but the top god is called Christos. The high priest lives at Rome. There was also another kind of god who created this world in six days. Anticipating your questions," she said, raising a paw to interrupt Kin, "I asked for more details. This creator-god has a lot of minor assistant gods with wings, and there's another lesser being called Saitan who sounds like an agitator. There's a lot of other usual religious stuff too."

"Six days is too fast," said Kin. "It's take the Company six years, even with prefabricated parts. Frankly, I'd put it all down as a myth."

"It's unusually straightforward," Silver pointed out. "In most myths the world is usually made from the supreme being's step-father's pancreas or the blood of the sacred beetle or something."

Kin frowned. Earth had plenty of religions, and had exported as many as she had imported. For every sect of humans engaged in complicated Ehftnic time rituals there was a group of saffron-dyed shandi drumming and chanting through the frozen Shandi streets. Generally Company people, being in the creation business, didn't bother with religion or went along with something basic and noncontroversial, like Wicca or Buddhism.

Kin had drunk of many cups in her time, just out of curiosity. Stand up, kneel down, climb a mountain, chant, go naked, whirl, dance, fast, abhor, gorge, pray—sometimes it was enjoyable, but it was always introverted, unreal.

Leiv's father spoke at length to one of the priests, who spoke to Silver. Silver laughed and replied.

"He wants to buy the Valhalla oven," she translated.

"The what?"

"The dumbwaiter. He says that he knows that in Valhalla all men eat and drink endlessly and now he knows it is because they have these ovens that grind out food and drink."

"Tell him it's not for sale." She looked directly at Eirick Raude. Red Eric. Back on Earth there was a worn mound in the heart of Valhalla where the water from the five inland seas spilled over into the Long Fjord. Eirick's Beard, they called the water. Red Eric had been buried in the mound. It was a big tourist attraction.

Silver took a deep breath.

"He also wants us to adjust the sun," she said. The man, seeing Kin's face, began to speak slowly in Latin.

"There has been spring in winter, he says. The sun has sometimes dimmed. On several nights the stars have flickered. And, uh, something happened to one of the planets."

Kin stared. Then she walked into the hall where Silver

had deposited the dumbwaiter and dialed for a big cup of the sweet ale. She brought it back and put it in Eirick's scarred hands.

"Tell him that was our fault. Tell him that if only we can learn the secrets of the world, we will replace the planet and do what we can about the sun. Did he say the stars *flickered*?"

"Apparently this is expected. The aforesaid Christos was born almost a thousand years ago, and it is widely believed that he will come again around about now. Take a look at the sea, will you?"

Kin turned. The waves were lashing at the beach, even here. She could hear the thunder of the storm out in the open sea. But the sky was blue, windless. . . .

"I said the disc wasn't a reliable artifact," she said. "It sounds like its governing systems are going wrong. Eirick doesn't seem all that worried, Silver."

"He says he's seen and heard of a lot of gods. He can take gods or leave them alone. If we can repair the weather, he will give us much timber."

"Timber?"

Silver turned to look at the village. "It seems to be a scarce commodity here," she said. "Notice the lack of trees."

This should be the Climatic Optimum, Kin told herself. On Earth it had been. The northern expansion had taken place during a long warm spell, when even a strip of coastal Greenland was reasonably habitable. . . .

Here, on some nights, the stars flickered out.

Marco and Kin spent the night in the hall, although Silver opted for the chill air of the boat. No one had attempted to bundle Kin off with the women. Goddesses were different.

She lay looking at the glow of the fire. The boom of the surf was still loud. Tides, she thought. That half-pint moon couldn't cause them. There must be some sort of regulated rise and fall of the sea, and it's going haywire.

She longed for a sleepset. They left your mouth tasting like an ape's urinal, but they were quick. You didn't suffer from insomnia with a zizz, or get bothered by rocks sticking in your back. A short, deep, dreamless sleep.

Finally she gave up, got up and walked through the darkened hall. The man at the door moved aside hastily to let her pass.

The sky was ablaze with fake stars. Kin shivered, but couldn't help but admire the ersatz universe that blazed over the dark, sea-noisy fjord.

This wasn't Earth. It was a disc about fifteen thousand miles across, massing around 5.67×10^{21} tons. That meant it either had generated gravity or neutronium veneer as a bedrock. It spun very slowly, like a tossed coin in treacle, dragging with it a fake sun and a fake moon and a family of fake planets. She knew all that, but sitting here it was hard to believe.

She shivered as the frost clawed at her. Frozen starlight.

A clockwork world. A world without astronomy. Maybe there was astronomy, but it was a horrible joke on the astronomers. A world where the venturesome dropped into the abyss. Dragons. Trolls. A myth-mash.

She found a planet, near what for want of a better word had to be called the disc's horizon. No, it was moving too fast for a planet.

And then it was suddenly a pennant of fire in the sky.

It hit the disc somewhere to the east. Kin told herself she could feel the impact.

She ran toward the line of beached ships to where a broad shape glittered with frost.

"Silver?"

Foolish, foolish. How many shandi on the disc?

"Ah, Kin. No doubt you saw it."

"What was it?"

"Most of the main part of our ship. It was only a matter of time. Marco should have exploded it rather than just leave it, and we can only hope it landed in the sea or a desert. I was hoping it would impact on the underside of the disc."

"It's certainly a good way of saying 'We're here' to any disc lords. First we take out a planet, then we drop our ship on them," said Kin.

"I noticed something before I saw the ship," said Silver. "See that planet, right down there? What would that be?"

"If this was Earth, that'd be Venus in that posi—no, it—"

"Quite so. It is moonless."

Kin felt a tingle of excitement. The disc builders had forgotten something. How could they? Venus and Adonis, a moon almost as big as Lunar, had always dominated

Earth's dawn or sunset sky. Why leave out the moon in the disc universe? A mystery.

"One could write a filmy on astronomy and sociology," said Silver. "For example, I have always felt that humans were the first into space because of the continual reminder that in our universe everything orbits something.

"You always had that other double-world system in your sky to hint that not everything revolves around the Earth. Whereas we had the Twin, and the kung couldn't see the sky at all. Had your sister world not had her moon, I doubt if your history would have been quite so uncomplicated."

Together they sat and watched the moonless world sink in solitude in the faintly glowing sky. Kin snuggled against Silver's fur, and wondered whether the dumbwaiter would be safe. Probably. The men had a healthy respect for Marco.

Silver was thinking about the same thing, because she said, "Kin? Are you awake?"

"Unk."

"If the dumbwaiter misfunctions, you must promise me you will stun me and allow Marco to put me to death."

Kin sat up, grimacing in the darkness. "Certainly not. Anyway, how could we stun you?"

"You have a palm stunner on you at this moment. I have noticed it on several occasions," said Silver. "I was taught to observe. You will kill me, for fear of what I will become. My fear."

Kin grunted noncommittally and lay back, thinking about shandi.

They couldn't take kung or human proteins. Before the dumbwaiters were common, it meant that shandi could only go offworld with a personal deep-freeze.

There had been a time when a human ship had been ferrying four shandi ambassadors to Greater Earth and the freezer malfunctioned. The ambassadors were civilized. Usually, when a shand was deprived of food, it turned into a ravening animal within two days. A million years of evolution was drowned in a wash of saliva.

With the ambassadors, it took fifty-six hours.

None survived. The last one took her life after awakening from a bloated sleep and seeing what lay around her in the cabin. The average shand wouldn't have done so, but the average shand was not an ambassador trained to think in cosmospolitan ways.

The plain truth was that the shandi liked eating shand. Can you fit ritual cannibalism into a civilization? They did.

There was the Game. The rules were ancient, venerated and simple. Two shandi enter, from opposite sides, a stretch of tundra or forest set aside for the purpose. There were special rules about weapons. The winner ate well.

Curiosity overwhelmed Kin.

"Did you ever play the Game, Silver?" she asked softly.

"Why, yes. Three times, when the urge was strong in my mouth," said the shand. "Twice at home, and once illegally elsewhere. My opponent in the latter case was the Regius Professor of Linguistics at the University of Gelt. Much of her stocks my freezer at home even now. I grieve that her death may largely have been in vain."

"But you've got dumbwaiters now. There's no need for the Game."

Silver shrugged. "Now it is a tradition," she said. "What we did out of need we do for . . . sport, I think it would be called, although there are elements of bravado, identification with our ancient past, the affirming of our shandness. You think this is barbaric."

It was a statement, not a question. Kin shook her head anyway.

"Some humans have taken part in the Game," said Silver. "They pay highly for the chance to prove their . . . what? Machismo? If they win, all they get is the head of their victim to hang on the wall. *That* is barbaric."

"Uh, what happens if the shand wins?"

"She gets two convicted criminals."

Kin thought: This is what shandi do on their home world, and none of your business. You can't apply humans' values to aliens. But you keep trying.

The train of thought was derailed by a scream from the big hall. A man burst out into the starlight and tumbled over on the grass, clutching at his side.

Kin landed running, snatching the stunner from her belt. She heard the heavy crash on the shingle as Silver landed behind her.

The hall was full of dark fighting shapes. Kin jerked aside as a leather-clad man ran out, followed by a tall man hefting an ax. She pointed the stunner and fired.

The effect was not immediate. The two kept on running. Then their legs collapsed under them in slow motion, and they hit the ground asleep.

Kin entered the hall with the stunner turned to minimum-power maximum-beam, swinging it like a scythe. A fighter staggered toward her with a raised sword and began to dream on his feet, sending her sprawling as fifteen stone of Norseman cannoned into her. For a moment she suffocated in a reek of stale sweat and badly tanned hides, then managed to roll away. The stunner was gone, dropped in the collision. She was in time to see a teetering giant pick it up curiously and look down the barrel. In the middle of the tumult, a look of perfect peace passed over his face. He fell like a tree.

Another man rushed at Kin. She kicked out and upward, and was rewarded with seeing his eyes cross before he rolled over, screaming and clutching his groin.

There wasn't a fight going on, it was a brawl. Most of the men were simply backing blindly at everything.

She managed to get to her feet, almost slipping on the curiously muddy floor. Through a gap in the figures she saw Marco dodging like a demon in the torchlight, a sword in all four hands. The dumbwaiter hummed behind him, a sticky, sweet smell in the air.

There was a bellow from the door and Eirick hobbled in, his face contorted with rage. He was flailing about with his crutch.

Then the roof fell in. One of the fighters backed into Kin, and she felled him with a backhanded chop as dawn-pale light flooded the hall. Part of the nearest wall bowed inward and crumbled away. There was a brief glimpse of a wide, white-haired foot.

Silver appeared at the roof hole, black against the gold sky. There was silence, broken only by the whimpers of the wounded and a background trickle.

Silver roared again. There was a brief moment of pandemonium as those who could rushed for the doorway.

Kin looked down. She was standing ankle-deep in a sticky, frothy puddle.

She looked at the dumbwaiter. A yellow-brown waterfall was spilling out of the food hatch, filling a deepening puddle. Marco looked at her, trying to focus. Then he sighed contentedly, and fell backward.

Resignedly, knowing what to expect, Kin held her cupped hand under the stream and tasted it. It was sweet and potent, a super-beer. Here and there in the pool, darker stains were spreading from the wounded and dying.

Kin stopped the flow and set the machine to producing an antidote. When it delivered a bowl of foul blue liquid she dragged the kung up by his comb, tipped the bowl into his mouth in one motion, and let him fall back into the mire.

After Silver dropped through the ruined roof she and Kin toured the hall. The 'waiter was instructed to produce the various seal-and-heal ointments in its repertoire, and after some thought Kin dialed for limb-replacement stimulants. Usually such sophisticated medicine was frowned on for its cultural shock effects, but hell, the disc was one big cultural shock. With some of the wounded she plastered the stuff on like mud, and hoped.

After a while Marco groaned and sat up. He looked at them hazily. Kin ignored him.

"Leiv's men told them about the 'waiter producing alcohol," he said thickly. "Then when I gave them a demonstration they began acting irrationally and demanding more. And then they started fighting."

"A fucking Valhalla machine," muttered Kin, and turned back to her work.

There was a hoarse chuckle from the darkness under the roof, and a black feather floated down.

They left at noon. The colony gathered to see them off.

Many of the men had new white scars. Some displayed tiny limbs already growing from healed stumps. But several had died in the hall; the Valhalla machine had been too efficient.

Eirick made a long speech in Latin and produced rare furs and two white hunting birds as farewell gifts.

"Say we can't accept," said Kin. "Say anything. We can't afford to carry the weight. Say we can't go and repair the sun if we carry too much weight. It's almost true."

Eirick listened to Silver's careful reply, and nodded graciously.

"I'd like to give him something, though," said Kin.

"Why?" snapped Marco.

"Because she's still afraid the Company might be behind

the disc, and she wants to apologize. Isn't that right?" said Silver. Kin ignored her.

"Ask him for some timber," she said. "Scraps. And grass or hay. Old bones. Anything that was living. What I have in mind'll mean the 'waiter will want feeding."

They set the dumbwaiter up as a timber mill. After the first meter of fragrant, smooth plank had been extruded from the hatch the colony worked like robots. Great drifts of seaweed, washed up by the pounding sea, helped swell the heap by the input hopper. Today the sea moved like liquid mountains.

Kin took the others aside while the colony was carting planks.

"We fly," she said. "Over land as much as possible, but we fly. If the belt power looks like running out before we get to the hub, then we'll charge up one belt from the others and Marco or I will go on alone. That means Silver can stay with the 'waiter."

"I am inclined to agree," said Silver. "There can be nothing to lose. Marco should be the one to go on, of course. I am big enough to scare predators, and you can survive by engaging any male humans in sexual congress if necessary. Marco is best equipped to reach the hub."

It was an elephantine attempt at diplomacy, but Marco turned his head away.

"I am equipped for nothing," he said distantly. "I allowed myself to be provoked by humans. I am shamed."

"The blame is not wholly yours," said Silver generously.

"But Silver, *I outnumbered them one to thirty*!"

Spray flew like sleet over the village. A respectable pile of planks had grown around the dumbwaiter. Kin switched it off and adjusted its lift belt.

The two Christos priests were standing apart from the crowd, chanting in Latin.

"What're they saying?" said Kin.

Silver listened for a moment. "It's an invitation to Christos to allow us to repair his planets and sun or alternately to strike us down if, as they suspect, we're servants of Saitan."

"Nice of them. Say goodbye for us, will you?"

They rose quickly. The huts and then the beach were lost against the background of snow and foam-topped sea.

The sea had gone mad. Waves piled on top of one another and burst and roared, sending spray almost as high as the flyers.

On the disc east couldn't be a direction, it had to be a point of the circumference. There were four directions on the disc: circle right, circle left, in, out. They headed *in.*

They circled the thing in the water carefully. Was it alive, Kin wondered, or was it just that the waves made it appear so? Once, a flipper broke water and slapped down again.

She decided to go lower. She waited for warnings from Marco, but he had been subdued all day. Silver said nothing, but took advantage of the midair stop to reel in the 'waiter on its towline.

Kin thought she could feel the cold air through the suit's twenty-five layers as she dived. The sky was pure blue, ice-clean.

The creature was floating belly upward. Most of it was tail, which snaked back until it was lost in surf. When a particularly heavy swell moved the body, Kin glimpsed a long equine head and one empty eyesocket.

It must have been old. No creature could grow that big fast. And the white belly was pitted with seaworm holes and studded with shellfish.

She flew back up. It would be nice to get it on a dissecting table—with a winch.

"It's dead," she announced. "There's a gash in it you could sail a boat through. Fresh, too. It's the same sort of creature as the one we saw this morning, I think."

It had been far to the right, looping through the water like a scaly-backed sine wave.

"It's very definitely dead," she said reassuringly, seeing Silver's face.

"What is currently occupying my mind is what killed it," said the shand. "I will be happy to get my feet on terra firma."

The more firmer the less terror, thought Kin. She found she preferred the sky. There was something reassuring about lift belts, far more so than the disc. She knew belts didn't fail. The disc might break up at any moment, but she would remain safely hanging in space.

"There is an island a few miles off," said Silver. "Just a dome of rock. I can see the marks of fires. Shall we land?"

Kin peered ahead. There was a smudge, a long way off. The sea seemed to be calm, too. The idea of a short stop had merit. The flying suits had never been designed for extended use in gravity. Her legs had been trailing uselessly below her since they left the settlement, and felt like lead. It would be nice to stamp some new blood into them.

"Marco?" she said. He was hovering some way off, still wrapped in self-recrimination.

There was a sigh in her ear. "I can hold no useful opinions," he said, "but I see no obvious dangers."

The island was small and obviously tidal. Seaweed, now almost dry, covered most of it. So many fires had been lit at the highest point of the rock, about three meters above the sea now, that it was black.

Kin landed first, and keeled over as her legs refused to support her. A crab scuttled out of the seaweed in front of her face.

Silver landed lightly and then hauled on the line to tow the dumbwaiter out of the sky. While Kin sat massaging some life back into her legs the shand bustled around cutting seaweed for the machine's intake hopper. In normal use the dumbwaiter extracted all its molecules from the air around it, but Silver had a big appetite.

After a while she tapped Kin on the shoulder and handed her a cup of coffee, reserving a large bowl of something red for herself. It was quite possibly synthetic shand. So what?

"Where's Marco?" said Kin, looking around. Silver swallowed and pointed upward.

"He's switched off his transmitter," she said. "He has problems, that one."

"You're not kidding," said Kin. "He thinks he's a human and knows he's a kung. And every time he acts like a kung he feels ashamed."

"All kung and humans are crazy," said Silver conversationally. "He's craziest. If he thought about it he would realize there's a logical impossibility about all this."

"Oh, yes," said Kin wearily. "I know he's not *physically* human, but the kung believe one's being is determined by the place—" She stopped. Silver was grinning encouragingly, and nodding.

"Go on," she said. "You're nearly there. Kung think the nearest available soul enters the offspring at birth. But Marco is supposed to be human. Humans don't really believe that kind of superstition, do they? Ergo, he must be a body-and-soul kung."

There was a gasp in Kin's ear. Marco may have switched off his transmitter, but kung were paranoid. He'd never switch off his receiver. Kin looked up at the distant dot in the air. Silver mouthed the words: Ignore him.

"I suppose Leiv's people lit those fires," said Kin vaguely. "We must be on a trade route."

"Yes. Have you noticed the variations in the sea's roughness?"

Kin had.

There were billions of tons of water on the disc, constantly draining over the edge. It had to get back somehow. Assuming the disc builders couldn't work magic, there was a molecule sieve down there, connected to—Kin writhed—a matter transmitter. Simple. You clamp receivers to the sea floor and pump the water back, only things were going wrong.

Over the last day and a half they had passed over circular areas of raging sea. Too much was coming up, or maybe only a few receivers were still available to take the volume.

"I keep forgetting this is just a big machine," she said.

"I think you are being too hard on the disc builders," said Silver. "Apart, of course, from the possibilities of a breakdown, there is no great disadvantage to living in a cosmos like this, surely? You can still evolve a science."

"Sure. The wrong science. Science is supposed to be the tool with which you can unscrew the universe, but disc science is only fit for the disc. It'd be closed, stagnant. Try to imagine a sophisticated disc astronomer trying to figure our sort of universe! The disc is only good for religions."

Silver dialed herself another bowl of goo. When she looked back Kin was shrugging out of her suit.

"Do you think that is wise?"

"Almost certainly not," said Kin, swaying slightly as a swell caught them. "But I'm damned if I'm going to sweat in there all day long. I'd give a handful of Days for a hot bath."

She walked naked toward the water and stopped abruptly as another swell nearly made her miss her footing.

On an island?

Marco dived out of the sky, screaming in Kung. A wave washed over Kin's feet, and as she turned the next one came in waist high and knocked her over. Through stinging spray she saw Silver and the dumbwaiter rocket out of the surf.

Cold water rolled over her. She groped in the green, ear-blocking light and managed to grab the fabric of the suit. It dragged at her as the dead weight of the lift belt pulled it down.

Beside her the water exploded into bubbles. Marco thrashed past, and there was a horrible moment before the suit pulled again—upward.

Silver was waiting. As the suit came up with Kin gripping it desperately she drifted closer. Marco surfaced in a rosette of foam.

"No!" he screamed. "Height! Get height! We're too near the sea!"

The grim pantomime started again two hundred meters up. With Silver holding Kin by the shoulders and Marco arranging the suit, they managed to slot her into the lower section, then forced her freezing arms into the sleeves. The inner thermal suit clicked on; by the time Kin was fit to talk the inside of the suit was a turkish bath.

"Thanks, Marco," she said. "You know, I never would have had the intelligence to switch—"

"Look below," said the kung.

They looked.

A shadow moved under the sunlit waves, a big turtle, island-sized, with four paddle legs and a head the size of a small house. As they watched it flapped lazily into the depths.

"I saw it wake," said Marco. "I had been pondering the regularity of the legs, wondering if they were shoals, and then one moved. No doubt it makes a practice of this and feeds on the unfortunates who light fires on its shell."

"A carapace length of a hundred meters," mused Silver. "Remarkable. Do such exist on Earth, Kin?"

"No," said Kin, through chattering teeth.

"Enough of this scientific chitchat," said Marco. "We must make speed for the nearest landmass. Silver, will you look yonder? About out-by-right, middle heaven. I only see a dot."

Silver turned her suit.

"It's a bird," she said. "Black. Possibly a raven."

"Then at least we cannot be far from land," said Marco. "I was afraid it was a dragon."

They switched the belts to maximum horizontal motion and headed on. Imperceptibly Marco pulled ahead, so that they traveled in delta formation. Kin assisted by slowing her suit fractionally, and noticed that Silver had done the same. Marco the kung was in command.

After a while he started to climb, the others following obediently. Below . . .

. . . the disc unfolded. At their old height Kin could have believed they were on a globe, but now the disc spread out below them for what it was—a lunatic map, a madman's Great Circle projection.

Cloud and the opacity of the air were the only barriers to vision. Kin could see the far rim of the disc, a darker line against the sky, and from the distant confusion of earth and sky two white horns grew and spread outward. The waterfall. The oceanfall, encircling the disc like a snake.

There was a hurricane building up, off the coast of Africa. As Kin climbed she watched the frozen spiral of cloud, fascinated.

She had seen worlds from space, but the disc was *different*. And it was big. She was used to thinking in terms of millions, and the disc, spinning through space inside its own private universe, had sounded small. Seen from a few hundred miles up it was huge, real. It was the light-years of nothingness that were small and meaningless. It was enough now just to stare. . . .

"Note the circles of disturbance in the ocean," said Marco.

"Kin suggests there is something the matter with the mechanism that recirculates the seawater," said Silver.

"Logical. Certainly I feel increased admiration for a people who face all this in small boats, with no air support."

Silver said, "Seeing the disc like this, one feels one would be nervous of setting foot on it again. It is too thin, too artificial. We do not as a rule suffer from vertigo, but seeing the disc like this I begin to comprehend what it means."

Marco nodded. "Quite so. It gives one an uneasy feeling around the ankles, akin to standing on a ledge a hundred stories up—a wide ledge perhaps, but a high one."

"I begin to see what Kin meant when she wrote about the Spindles' insistence on having a few thousand miles of planet beneath their feet," said Silver. "It is a mental anchor. The subconscious fears the endless drop toward the bottom of the Universe. Could our vague feeling be a shadow of the Spindle imperative?"

"It is said that they helped us evolve, so that is always possible. What do you think, Kin? *Kin?*"

"Hunh? Wassat?"

"Were you listening?"

"Sorry, I was looking at the scenery. Silver, what's that smudge down there? In what would be Central Europe."

"I see it. That, I suspect, is where our ship crashed."

They all looked. The smoke was a mere wisp at this distance.

"It looks like a pretty lifeless region," said Silver, in tones of comfort.

"It is now," said Kin bitterly.

Invisible a few miles below, its wings a blur of speed, the raven focused on the smoke. Behind its eyes, something went click.

The moon rose, full but reddish, underpowered. It illuminated a speeding landscape that was mainly forest. Here and there patches of land and a few orange lights indicated a settlement.

Marco called them to a halt after a long stretch of dark forest roof had passed below.

"Marco, let's land," said Kin wearily.

"Not until we have spied out the land!"

"That bit immediately below us looks unmatched, believe me."

Silver landed first, on the reasonable assumption that wild animals would be unlikely to attack her. She switched off her suit and unzipped the helmet, then stood silently, nostrils dilating. After a minute she turned, sniffed again.

"It's okay," she said. "I smell wolves, but the scent is old. There are some boars about a mile hubward, and I think there's some beavers in that river about two miles toward the rim. No men." She sniffed again, and hesitated. "There is something else. Can't identify it, though. Odd. Vaguely insectile."

They landed anyway. Kin was dozing in her suit, but concentrated just long enough to stop the belt from crashing her into the turf at the side of the hill. She switched off, and allowed herself to sink gently into the scented grass.

She awoke when Marco gently put a bowl of soup into her hands.

He and Silver had lit a fire. Orange flames shot up and illuminated the forest leaves thirty meters away, and made the camp a circle of comforting firelight. It glittered off the dumbwaiter

"Who should know better than I that it is unsafe?" said the kung, seeing the questioning look in her face. "But I'm human enough to say what the hell. Silver has taken first watch. Then it's you. Better get some more sleep."

"Thanks. Uh, look, Marco, about that floating island—"

"We will not mention it. We will be over land most of the rest of the way to the hub."

"We may find nothing."

"Of course. But what is all life but a journeying toward the Center?"

"I'm more worried about the belt power sources. Can we be sure they'll last out?"

"No, but there is a built-in hysteresis effect. If the power sinks below a certain level it'll waft you gently to the ground."

"Or the sea," said Kin.

"Or the sea. But I know what is worrying you. It is the fear that your Company did all this. But why should they?"

"Because we can."

"I don't understand."

"No. But we could build dragons, we could create people in the vats so easily as we breed up extinct whales. The theory is all there, but we don't do it because of the Code. *But it is possible.* We could have built this disc, but no one would dare do it in home space. Out here—it's a different matter."

Marco looked at her sadly. "Silver convinced me," he said. "If I'm rational, I'm a kung. I'm *glad* I'm not human."

Kin finished her soup and lay back. She felt warm and full. Marco had curled up with four Norse swords beside him, but she could dimly make out Silver sitting motionless higher up the hill. Always a comforting sight, she told herself. As long as the dumbwaiter works.

* * *

She did not dream.

Silver shook her awake before midnight. Kin yawned and staggered to her feet.

"Anything been happening?" she mumbled.

Silver considered. "I think an owl hooted about an hour ago, and there were some bats. Apart from that, it has been pretty quiet."

Silver lay down. Within a few minutes deep snores told Kin she was on her own.

The moon was high, but still too red. The stars had taken on that deep light that always comes around midnight. Grass, heavy with dew, rustled as she walked away from the dying fire.

Even now there was still some light on the sunset rim, a green glow that just managed to delineate the boundary between disc and sky. Moths hummed past her face, and there was a smell of crushed thyme.

Later, she wondered if she had dozed on her feet. But the moon was still up and the—call it the west—was still a line of faint luminosity. Yet the music came pouring down the hillside confidently, as though it had been there all the time.

It thrilled, then soared into a few bars of evocative melody. Evocative of what, Kin could not decide—perhaps of things that never were, but which ought to have been. It was distilled music.

The fire was a sullen eye between the two sleeping figures. Kin started to climb the bare hill, leaving darker footprints in the damp grass.

A picture came into her mind of the music as a living thing, coiling around the hill and disappearing into the hushed forest. She told herself she could always turn back if she wanted to, and walked on.

She saw the elf on a mossy stone at the top of the hill, outlined against the afterglow. It sat cross-legged, hunched over the pipes, intent upon the music.

Inside the woman who stood entranced, another Kin Arad, imprisoned in the corner of the mind, hammered on the consciousness: (It's an insect! Don't listen! It looks like a cross between a man and a cockchafer! Look at the antennae! Those things aren't ears!)

The music stopped abruptly.

"No—" said Kin.

The triangular head turned round. For a moment Kin looked into two narrow, glittering eyes that were greener than the light behind them. Then there was a hiss and a patter of feet over the turf. A little later, there was a rustle in the forest. Then the night closed in again, like velvet.

At dawn they rose above the forest and headed hubward, leaving long curling trails in the rising mists.

On the horizon a pillar of smoke loomed like the finger of judgment. It was so thick it cast a shadow.

"I don't know what effect it has on the natives, but it terrifies me," said Kin. "We should have blown up the ship in the air, Marco."

"Their planet hit us," he said testily. "It is their responsibility."

The forest gave way to fields, striped with crops. A distant man, walking behind a plow drawn by ant-sized oxen, fell on his knees as their shadow passed over him. From the boundaries of the field a dirt road ran through a cluster of turf huts, forded a river and disappeared under the trees.

"He didn't look like a whizz planetary technician," said Kin.

"No," said Marco. "He looked shit-scared. But *someone* built this disc."

Breakfast they had on a cliff top overlooking the sea. Marco watched it carefully. After a while he asked: "Kin, if you were the disc master, how would you arrange for tides?"

"Easy. Have a water reservoir under the disc and occasionally allow extra water into the sea. Why?"

"This tide is bloody high. There are half-drowned trees down there. What is the matter? Are you being attacked?"

"Yes, and the sooner I can get a nice hot bath the better. With soap! Ever since Greenland I've been carrying passengers."

Marco looked blank. Kin sighed.

"Fleas, Marco. Irritating parasites. Right now I could forget about the Preservation of Extinct Species Law and kill the lot.

"And you can't scratch very well in a bubble suit."

Silver coughed. "I too would like the chance of some hygienic reparations," she said.

Marco finally consented to make an extended stop later in the day, after Kin announced that if he did not she would land outside the first building that looked like a tavern.

As they sped over the sea Silver added, "We are heading for Germany. Not a good place."

"Why?" asked Marco.

"A battleground. Danes spreading southward meeting Magyars heading westward and Turks heading everywhere, with the locals fighting everyone. According to history, that is."

"Anyone have an air force?"

"The technology was pri—"

"It was a joke."

Kin itched, and stared morosely at the sea. She thought she saw a boat, hull uppermost, rolling in the waves. They were past before she could take a closer look. But she was the first to see the rosette.

From above, the sea had put forth a flower, green petals edged with white. Losing altitude, they saw the mounds of water burst through the surface every few seconds and spread in a succession of roaring, concentric waves.

"Tide pump," said Marco, and flew on.

They crossed a wide beach, a checkerboard of fields, and a forest. And then a town—small, bucolic, but a town.

"The fortress I can recognize," said Marco, pointing to a squat stone building among the canted roofs, "but what is the large wooden construction?"

"Could it be a heated swimming pool?" murmured Kin. "Don't look at me like that. The Remens had hot baths."

"Romans," corrected Silver. Marco grunted and glided off, leaving them to chase after him.

"Why the big rush?" said Kin.

He pointed to the smoke column. Kin had to admit it was impressive, even at this distance.

"That's why," he said. "According to Silver the disc people are ripe for mob hysteria. What do you think they'd be doing now that's in their sky?"

They landed in a mixed forest well out of sight of habitation, where a stream flowed between low sandy banks.

Kin stripped off her suit as soon as she landed and, while Silver scrabbled at the sand, switched the dumbwaiter to one of its least-complicated settings. Soon it gushed hot water, filling the hole. She wallowed.

Marco prowled uneasily along the bank and disappeared up a steep, tree-shaded slope. A moment later he came bounding down.

"We must leave! There's a track up there!"

Silver looked at Kin and shrugged, then wandered up the slope. She came back looking thoughtful.

"There is a distant odor of humans," she said, "but it is a forest track, that's all, and there are plants growing undisturbed all over it."

They glared at Marco.

"People use it," he said. "They may have weapons."

"Only axes, I should think," said Kin. "Anyway, superstition will protect us. There are tidal forests on Kung, aren't there?"

"I understand so, yes."

"Well, what would be the reaction of a simple peasant kung forester who suddenly chanced upon strange and fearsome monsters in his forest?"

"He would fall upon them and destroy them utterly!"

Kin bit her lip. "I guess he would, at that. Well, humans are different. Don't worry."

Later she dialed for soap and did her laundry. Silver had paddled off downstream and found a deep pool, nicely cold, in which she was floating contentedly. Marco relaxed sufficiently to bathe his broad feet in the stream.

There was a sudden movement in the water and he hissed shrilly, jumping up and landing ready to fight. Kin watched wide-eyed, then reached down and quickly grabbed a small yellow frog.

She showed it to him without speaking. Marco glared. Finally Kin ran out of air and burst out laughing. The kung looked from her to the impassive frog, hissed menacingly, turned and stomped off along the riverbank.

That was unfair of me, she thought. Kung have no sense of humor, even kung brought up on Earth. She released the frog and paddled farther out into the stream.

It was clear, and slow enough for yellow water lilies to have established a roothold. Water boatmen rowed furiously underwater to escape her as she dived.

She drifted in the golden-brown water between the lily stalks, moving with just the faintest motion of wrists and ankles. There were ramshorn snails with red skin, and small fish darting like swallows in the shadowy cathedrals made by the weeds. . . .

She rose in a cloak of bubbles and surfaced in a clump of flowers, shaking the water out of her hair.

The archers were well disciplined. Kin looked at the row of arrow heads, wavering only slightly, and quickly decided against diving. Refraction of light or not, they could still hit her underwater.

There were eight archers in rough clothing and a haphazard assortment of armor and chain mail. They wore close-fitting metal helmets, and beneath them their blue eyes bored into Kin stolidly.

A voice was squeaking in her earpiece.

". . . and don't start anything stupid," it said. "There's too much risk of being hit. We must handle this carefully."

Kin looked around slowly. There was nothing to be seen downstream but stands of reed mace and thick bushes.

"I like the *we*," she said aloud.

"Just don't stare too intently at the big bush with the purple flowers," said Marco.

Before she could answer, a man pushed his way between the archers and grinned down at her.

He was short and built like a wall. Even his skin was brick-colored. A thatch of yellow hair and wide mustaches framed eyes that glittered enough to remind Kin that intelligence didn't necessarily start with an industrial revolution.

He wore leggings, a belted smock that fell to his knees, and a red cloak. They all looked as though they had been slept in, if not worse. One calloused hand tapped thoughtfully at the hilt of a half-concealed sword.

Kin smiled back.

Finally he stopped the grinning contest by kneeling down and extending a hand. Jewels gleamed on the dirt-ingrained fingers, with a suggestion that they had once belonged to other people.

Kin accepted the hand as gracefully as she could, and climbed out onto the bank. There was a faint sigh from the men. She treated them all to another smile, which caused them to step back uneasily, and plucked a water-lily flower from her hair.

Brickface broke the spell with an appraising glance and a short comment that caused a general snigger.

"Turn up the gain control," said the voice in her ear. "If he is speaking Latin, Silver may be able to translate."

"I don't need a translation of that," said Kin. She treated her audience to another toothpaste grin and stepped forward. Brickface nodded and one man darted hurriedly out of the way.

A group of three men were standing around the dumbwaiter. Two of them wore heavy gray robes and the third, a youth, wore clothes that were bright and obviously impractical. All three pulled back guiltily as she approached.

Then the youth said something and reached inside his shirt, pulling out an amulet which he held in front of him as he advanced stiff-legged toward her. He held it like a weapon. Kin noticed that his eyes were glazed. Swea glistened on his forehead.

He stopped in front of her, staring straight ahead. She sensed that everyone was expecting something of her.

She reached out gingerly and took the amulet.

There was a gasp from the robed pair. Behind he Brickface doubled up with sudden laughter. The youn man stared, lips moving on soundless words. Kin peere politely at the thing in her hands. It was a wooden cross with what she at first thought was the figure of an acroba she handed it back as graciously as she could manage.

The young man grabbed it, looked frantically around th clearing, and scurried away up the slope to the track.

As the robed men started to follow him Kin could se what they had been doing. They had run a sword into th dumbwaiter's output slot.

"They're breaking up the 'waiter!" she hissed.

"Okay, Kin. When I say duck, duck. DUCK!"

Something whirred past her head and struck one of th men between the eyes. He gave a sigh and topple backward.

"*Cape illud, fracturor,*" said a satisfied voice in her ea Brickface gripped her wrist firmly and stalked toward th slope, the archers following him as closely. They glance fearfully at the forest.

"What was that?" said Kin as she was jerked up th slope. Pine needles clung and pricked her feet.

"Silver threw a stone," said Marco, the awe in his voi recognizable even in a earpiece reproduction. Kin look back and saw the 'waiter, her suit and the fallen man lying forlornly near the water's edge.

"There is little we can do at present," said the kung conversationally. "The weaponry is laughable, but the situation is not sufficiently desperate to warrant a direct confrontation."

"Uh?"

"I would not wish you to think that I am motivated by anything other than intelligent caution."

"No, Marco."

"Now Silver would like a word." There was a rustle.

"You are thought to be some kind of water spirit," said Silver. "Apparently they are not uncommon. You should have screamed when they showed you that figure of the Christos. My immediate advice is to cover yourself as soon as possible. There appears to be some rigid prohibition concerning nudity."

There were more armed men waiting on the track, with some robed men among them. Brickface swung himself into the saddle of a waiting horse and lifted Kin up behind him, dumping her on the beast's rump without a word and then ignoring her. At his brief command the entire troop moved off.

"This is Silver again. Do not despair."

"I am not despairing," said Kin. "I am just getting good and mad."

"We have returned to the clearing. Marco is reviving the stunned priest." There was a thin scream which stopped abruptly. "Kin?"

"I'm still here," she said. One of the robed men had ridden up alongside Brickface. He wore a fur-edged cloak over his robe and appeared to be important. He was also furious.

"This is a perfect opportunity," said Silver. "Hopefully we shall shortly learn more about these people. If you find yourself in difficulties, you can of course initiate sexual relations with your captor. The men call him Lothar."

The cloaked man was shouting and pointing back along the trail, with occasional poisonous looks at Kin. Lothar's replies were distant and monosyllabic, until he reached over and in one movement grabbed the priest by the front of his robe and almost lifted him off his horse. He snarled a sentence and spat a full stop. The other man went white, out of either fury or fear.

"This is exceptionally interesting," said Silver. Kin thought she could also hear a babble of high-pitched Latin in the background.

"Is the 'waiter badly damaged?" said Kin.

"Not badly. It can be repaired. Another centimeter and the sword would have hit the five-thousand-kilovolt line—*Marco*!It is essential he does not faint again!"

The party left the forest and headed hubward by Kin's estimation, on a track that ran alternately between stretches of half-cultivated ground and marshes.

The smoke pillar loomed, dominating the sky. Its tip was now made ragged by high-altitude winds.

Soon they met a straggle of people coming the other way. They ran off the track when they saw Lothar's band, but he wheeled after them and one man was caught. He was brought before Lothar, struggling and gasping out answers to the questions that were grunted at him.

"Silver," said Kin, "how do you say 'I'm nearly freezing to death'?"

Silver translated. Kin tapped Lothar on the shoulder and repeated the phrase, as best she could.

He turned in the saddle and stared at her in astonishment, before unfastening the heavy brooch that held his cloak. Kin wrapped the heavy and odorous cloth around her. There was a comment, almost inaudible, from the senior priest.

"He said, 'Soon you will both be warmed by the fires of Hell,' " murmured Silver helpfully.

"Great. I've only been here a few hours and already I've made friends."

"Listen carefully. Your party contains priests of the Christ-Creator religion. They are heading toward the smoke column in the belief that it is a sign that the Christ has returned. Lothar, however, is a minor noble with a line in brigandage and part-time looting. According to our information, he is a son of Saitan."

"Saitan has a lot of relatives in these parts," said Kin.

"It is a strange religion. Everyone is evil until proved holy. Our informant says the priests met up with Lothar on the road and they banded together for mutual protection, but this liaison is likely to end at any moment."

"Are you telling me that Lothar's God is returning and he's thinking of nothing but pillage?"

"Probably rape and murder as well," said Silver. "You are heading for a holy house for the night. We will endeavor to rescue you then. Now I must sign off for the moment, I've got an injured man to attend to. I'll say this for these Christers, they're brave. This one hit out at Marco. Picture the result."

"Dead?"

"I persuaded Marco that the man was more useful alive. He just broke both his arms."

In the early evening they came to a town of thatched houses surrounding what Silver identified as a religious foundation. The muddy streets were thick with people and carts. The party got through only after Lothar sent men ahead to clear a path with the flats, and sometimes the points, of their swords.

There were noisy crowds around the holy buildings, dressed in the main in drab and holy colors. The senior priest was greeted effusively, even frantically, and helped to dismount. Lothar watched impassively. Looking around, Kin saw that his men had fanned out among the crowd with drawn bows, sometimes glancing at the sky.

The senior priest, identified by Silver as Otto, spoke sharply to a holy man. He ran off and returned a few minutes later a respectful distance in front of one who, to judge by the way the crowd parted for him, was even holier.

He was tubby and red-eyed, as if he hadn't slept for some time. Over the standard robe he wore a red cloak with patterns in gold thread, now crusted with dirt. He listened gravely as Otto spoke. Then he walked over to Lothar's horse and peered at Kin. Finally he reached out and pinched her sharply on the thigh.

In the circumstances, she decided against any action.

Lothar dismounted and fell on one knee in front of the priest, one hand on his heart. He spoke eloquently. To Kin he sounded like a salesman.

She tried to raise Silver.

"I can be of little help," the shand reported. "Latin is a ceremonial language, like a religious allspeak. This is one of the early German tongues, I think. The fat man is possibly the local bishop, and this is a trial. What appears to be at stake is whether Lothar keeps you or hands you over."

"What about the heroic rescue? It's wearying, you know, constantly being tensed up waiting for one's friends to plummet out of the sky with lasers blazing—"

"I had intended using your stunner, but it was not in your suit," said Silver. "No doubt you lost it on the floating island. Plan B also will not work. Marco intended to swoop down wearing two belts and carry you off, but Lothar's men maintain a constant skywatch. For dragons, do you think?"

"What's plan C, then?"

There was a sigh. "Marco intends to land and hack and slash at everyone."

"That's a good plan," said Kin.

"He is mad. The Norsemen have a term, *berserker*. It was designed for Marco."

Lothar stopped speaking. The bishop looked down at him, then up at Kin. He beckoned.

After a few seconds she slid off the horse's back, the cloak slipping from her as she landed. There was a rustle of voices from the crowd.

The bishop nodded and waddled off, beckoning Kin to follow him. The crowd pressed in silently behind her.

They went between the holy buildings to a stamped-earth yard, full of long shadows in the sinking sun light. Part of the yard was roofed. Under the roof were bars.

"I'm about to be locked up, Silver!" she hissed. "Where the hell are you?"

"A wooded eminence outside the town. The bars do not look alarmingly thick. They may trust to them to guard you."

"Silver, how can you see the bars?"

"Marco is behind you in the crowd. He is giving me eyewitness reports. *Do not look for him.*"

The bishop stopped by the middle cage, and swung open the door. When Kin stopped there was the gentle prod of a sword in her back. She stepped in.

The lock was primitive but big. The bars did not look alarmingly thick, according to Silver. They were six-inch posts. What was normally kept there that needed six-inch-thick bars?

They left her sitting in the dirt and walked away. After a while the last of the crowd left the compound, leaving a group of bowmen who spread out, watching the sky. Presently a man brought her a bowl of scraps, dropped them within her reach, and bolted.

A few stars lit up. Beyond the compound's walls came the rattle of carts, and many shouts.

"Silver?" she said querulously.

There was a heart-stopping pause before the reply came back.

"Ah, Kin. I am now better informed. Your precise status is still to be determined. Your friend Lothar has at least saved you from arbitrary execution. I have also learned more about the current disc situation. Would you be interested in hearing it? We will not collect you until it is fully dark. I doubt if those bowmen can better Marco's excellent night vision."

"Go ahead and amuse me," said Kin, wrinkling her nose over the food bowl. It could make me sick, she decided; it looks as though it's already done so to someone else.

"This is all exceptionally interesting," said Silver. "There is no doubt among the populace that this is either the return of the Christ or the end of the disc or both. Fires are raging—our ship, you understand. There have been strange signs in the sky. The town is divided between travelers hastening to the advent and those fleeing from it."

Kin listened to the cries outside.

"What are they fleeing for?" she asked.

"He's a very choosy god."

"How did you find out about this?"

There was a pause. At last Silver said, "Promise me that if we get back home you won't reveal the information-gathering system we, uh, evolved. I could be subject to severe disciplinary action from the all-planet committee on anthropological research procedures."

"My lips are sealed," promised Kin.

"Marco slugs a likely-looking subject, flies him over here and knocks the shit out of him until I've heard enough."

Kin grinned. "It's not like drawing circles in the sand, is it?"

"Much more efficient, though."

There was a commotion at the entrance to the compound. In the half-light Kin saw a knot of men approaching, surrounding a taller shape that moved across the ground in hops.

When it drew nearer the cages Kin saw that it was roughly man-shaped but at least three meters high. Once it reared and spread a pair of dark wings the size of sheets. One of the men darted forward. The tall shape whimpered, and cowered. Kin, pressed against the bars, got an impression of scales, and pectoral muscles like barrels.

She jumped back as the door of the neighboring cage was opened and the thing prodded inside. She saw a stubby-horned head and glowing green eyes that narrowed when they saw her.

The door slammed shut and the men retreated quickly. The creature grunted, gave the door an experimental shake, went and sat down in the far corner of the cage with its arms around its knees.

The men returned, and they were carrying a small struggling body. Kin made out the shape of a creature like the one she had seen on the hilltop—part-human, part-animal, part-insect. It whistled shrilly as it was carried. As one of the men let go to reopen the cage door, it screeched and raked his chest with a claw. When he fell back it wriggled free, kicked another man in the stomach with a small hoof, and sank its teeth into a third's arm before it was grabbed.

The man who had been clawed stood up silently and landed a swinging blow that crunched when it hit, like the crushing of beetles. It landed in a heap inside the cage, and lay still.

The men retreated but did not leave the area. After a while a watchman's fire sprang up. Kin called up Silver.

"They are staying," she said. "There must be ten of them now. Marco'll never get in!"

"I think the guard is for the benefit of your friend in the next cell," said Silver. "Marco has a plan, though. Two plans, in fact. If the first doesn't work, he proposes to explode the 'waiter's powerpack."

Kin thought about it. "That would kill us all," she said, "and leave a crater about a mile across."

"Quite so. But we would have *won*."

There had never been a man-kung war, just a few early skirmishes now diplomatically forgotten. Kung had no concept of conquest, mercy, prisoners or rules. Marco was tainted with human ideas, but . . .

"Is he serious?"

"I think he is frightened almost to death."

The big winged creature was watching Kin. She was aware of two pale lights in the gloom.

"I have my own plan," said Silver.

"Oh, good. I like listening to plans."

"I have compiled a speech. When a priest next approaches you will recite it to him.

"You are an Ethiopian princess, left stranded in this country when your party was attacked by robbers. You demand to be released. You are a devout Christer, by the way. So is your father, who is a king, and who will be angry in very physical ways when he hears about this treatment."

"It sounds a bit contrived," said Kin. She was watching the giant in the next cell. Three meters high. What did it use for ankle bones?

"KIN ARAD," said the winged demon.

She stared. Nothing had moved. The creature was still slumped against the bars, watching her. When he spoke again—Kin couldn't be sure in the dim light, but the lip movements didn't seem to coincide with the sounds she heard, as if something was being badly dubbed.

"I am Kin Arad," she said.

"WHAT IS YOUR DOMINION?" said the demon in perfect allspeak.

"I don't know what you mean."

"I AM SPHANDOR, OF THE DOMINION OF AGLIERAP. I CANNOT DETERMINE YOUR DOMINION OR PLACE."

"It seems to be speaking shandi," said Silver.

"SPEAK, ARE WE PARTNERS IN ADVERSITY?"

"I hear it in allspeak," said Kin urgently. "I think it's using some kind of direct mind stimulation. Its lips aren't moving properly."

"DO NOT MUMBLE. DO YOU THINK I DO NOT KNOW OF THE CREATURES TO WHOM YOU TALK BY THE POWER OF THE LIGHTNING? THE THINKING BEAR AND THE UPRIGHT FROG WITH FOUR ARMS? AND THE MECHANICAL DEVICE THAT PREPARES FOOD BEYOND THE POWERS OF HUICTIIGRARAS?"

"Are you reading my mind?"

"OF COURSE I AM, YOU STUPID BITCH. BUT IT IS DIFFICULT. YOU ARE OF THIS WORLD YET NOT OF THIS WORLD, NEITHER ARE YOU OF THE BROTHERHOOD OF THE DAMNED. YET THE PRAYING ONES HAVE CAPTURED YOU."

"Keep it talking," said Silver.

"The Christers think I am a water sprite," said Kin.

"SPRITES CANNOT SPEAK AND ARE OF LOW INTELLIGENCE, AS EVERYONE KNOWS. THEY ARE LIKE THIS THING."

Sphandor kicked out and managed to hit the wheezing faun with a curbed toenail. It whimpered.

"It's injured," said Kin. "Can we do anything to help it?"

"WHY SHOULD WE? IT BARELY KNOWS IT IS ALIVE. ELVES BREED LIKE FLIES IN THE WOODS. YOU THINK THEY MAKE NICE MUSIC, BUT IT IS AS A CRICKET CHIRPS—MINDLESSLY.

"I GATHER YOU HAD SOMETHING TO DO WITH THE EXPLOSION THAT KNOCKED ME OUT OF THE AIR THREE DAYS AGO?"

"Uh, Yes." Kin thought quickly. "There was a flying chariot, you see—"

"A THREE-THOUSAND-TONNE STARSHIP," Sphandor agreed, "IMPACTING AT FOUR HUNDRED MILES AN HOUR."

"Do you know what those words mean?"

"NO, BUT THEY WERE AT THE FOREFRONT OF YOUR MIND. THE SHOCK WAVES KNOCKED ME OUT OF THE AIR, AND SOME CHRISTERS REACHED ME AND BOUND ME BEFORE I COULD RISE. IF I BUT HAD MY FREEDOM I WOULD TEAR THEIR EARS OFF."

It must be vat-grown, thought Kin. Nothing like that could have evolved naturally. If those wings worked it would have to be very light, bird-boned. She would have to ask it questions—later.

"I want to escape," she said. "Silver?" There was no answer from the earpiece.

"I LIKEWISE. IT IS UNFORTUNATELY IMPOSSIBLE. TOMORROW WE SHALL BE BROUGHT BEFORE THE BISHOP'S COURT. I SHALL CERTAINLY BE EXECUTED."

"Will they waste time with a court when they think their god is coming?"

"ALL THE MORE REASON TO BE SEEN GOING ABOUT WHAT THEY CONSIDER TO BE HIS BUSINESS, KIN ARAD."

"What will they execute you for?"

"I AM SPHANDOR! I SPREAD ARTHRITIS, THE BONEACHE AND AGUE OF THE NECK. I BLIGHT CROPS AND CAUSE ABORTION IN CATTLE. THEY SAY I FOUL STREAMS AND HURL THE LIGHTNING STONE."

"And do you do all that?"

"I SUPPOSE SO. I CERTAINLY ALWAYS INTEND TO."

Kin glanced toward the fire. The men had spread out, and she could just see them outlined against the last stains of sunset, watching the sky.

"THEY THINK MY BROTHERS WILL TRY TO RESCUE ME," said Sphandor. "FAT CHANCE!"

A holy man entered the compound with a tray of food. Kin watched him absently.

One of the guards sauntered over to the priest and took a bowl off the tray. He had his back to Kin, who saw him stiffen, drop the bowl and slump down. A third hand had shot out of the robe, holding a sword. . . .

Some of the others came running after hearing the priest's anguished cry, and the fallen man was lost to sight as his fellows gathered round.

There was an explosion of flesh.

Two men staggered back and two, a little faster, turned to run and slid along the ground with knives in their backs.

Laughing like a hyena, Marco leaped barehanded at the others. The few seconds of astonishment they experienced helped him, and he worked through them with a mixture of kung digitsju and blind destruction while arrows from the men who had the sense to stay out of it hissed around him. Sphandor giggled.

Marco screeched a kung battle cry and stalked toward the nearest archer, glistening in the firelight. The man fired one arrow which hit him fairly in the chest, rocking him back on his heels for a moment. Then he walked on. The archer was still staring when two hands grabbed him by the throat and two more swung up in a gristle-cleaving arc.

As one man the surviving guards dropped their weapons and ran for the compound entrance.

"Marco!" shouted Kin. "Keys! Find the keys."

Marco glared at her stupidly, then looked up. A white shape dropped out of the night, towing the familiar form of the dumbwaiter behind her.

Silver landed lightly. Behind her, Marco wrenched the arrow from his chest and looked at it absently.

"NEAT," commented Sphandor with interest.

The shand examined the cage closely.

"I do not like to damage private property," she said, "but speed is of the essence." She stepped back a few paces and hit the bars at a dead run. As Kin jumped over the debris the shand nodded toward Sphandor.

"What about that?" she said.

"I PLEAD," said the demon.

"Let him out," said Kin, taking her suit and stepping into the lift belt. "Right now I'd just love him to spread bubonic plague of whatever it is he spreads."

"Does he do that?" said Silver. "The ancients always said demons spread disease."

"This one is a mobile disaster area," said Kin.

"Is it wise to let him loose, then?"

"We might learn a lot from him. If you've got any scruples, remember Marco's just killed half a dozen men and you've been involved in the molestation of research subjects."

Silver considered this. "True," she said, and splintered the bars with a backhand swipe. "If we're baddies, let's be *bad*."

Marco stepped forward with two knives leveled to throw as the demon wriggled through the gap. There was a smear of pink blood around his wound. Would it have helped the dead archer to know that a kung in a fighting rage was practically awash with regenerative enzymes? It had been hard enough for Earthmen to see kung fight on with their flesh healing like boiling wax.

"I do not trust this creature. Grab him!"

Silver shot out an arm and caught Sphandor by his scaly tail. With the other hand she unwrapped a length of cable from her waist and knotted it several times around the creature's neck. Sphandor screeched.

"WHERE ARE YOU, SOIGNATORIE, UNSORE, DILAPIDATORE—" he began.

"Shut up," advised Marco, taking the other end of the cable from Silver. "All ready? Soon people will overcome their fears."

They rose quickly. Marco hovered fifty meters up and looked down at the demon, a tall shadow in the moonlight. Sphandor shrugged. The big wings unfolded.

"I SHALL REQUIRE A RUN TO TAKE OFF."

Kin watched Marco bob above him as the demon loped across the ground, the wide wings rattling. Halfway across he brought them down with a *whump* that threw up a dust cloud, and he hung there for several seconds while the wings hammered on the air. Then he rose ponderously, like a giant heron.

When he was level with them, but a hundred meters away, he took a length of cable in his talons.

"FAREWELL, FOOLS!" he bellowed, and tugged. A look of dismay crept over his face.

With the belt's lateral stabilizers full on Marco hung immovable in the air. When he reeled in the line no amount of wing flapping could budge him. When the horned head was just a few meters away the kung whispered. "I'm told you can read minds. . . ."

"ONLY SURFACE THOUGHT, LORD."

"Read mine."

After a second Sphandor's face was a mask of terror.

With the creature in tow they moved slowly, because the wide wings acted as an air brake. The demon held a loop of cable in both hands and glided behind them unsteadily, peppering them alternately with entreaties and curses.

The smoke no longer dominated the sky. It *was* the sky. Winds in the upper air had teased it out into a ragged mushroom.

Apart from the background noise behind them they flew in silence, Kin and Silver following a little behind Marco. Finally Kin's radio chimed.

"This is Silver, transmitting on your suit frequency only, Kin. You had something to say? If you move the switch to position four Marco will not hear," the voice added.

"Silver, he slaughtered them! They didn't have a chance!"

Silver made a noncommittal noise. "They outnumbered him ten to one."

"They weren't expecting a kung, damm it!" Kin felt the bottled-up words rushing to be said. "He enjoyed it! You saw him, he even killed ones who were running away, he threw . . . their only crime was that they happened to be in his way, it was completely inhu—" She choked on the word.

After a while Silver said: "Quite."

Kin thought about the first contact with the kung. Men had already met the shandi, who apart from their dueling had no concept of warfare and viewed mankind's ragged history with barely concealed horror. So the first ship to land on Kung had no weapons aboard at all.

Five deaths served to convince men that, considered on the galactic scale, they were gentle and peace-loving. Perhaps it had been worth it.

"We all think we understand each other," Kin heard Silver say. "We eat together, we trade, many of us pride ourselves on having alien friends—but all this is only possible, only possible, Kin, because we do not fully comprehend the other. You've studied Earth history. Do you think you could understand the workings of the mind of a Japanese warrior a thousand years ago? But he is as a twin to you compared with Marco, or with myself. When we use the word 'cosmopolitan' we use it too lightly—it's flippant, it means we're galactic tourists who communicate in superficialities. We don't *comprehend*. Different worlds, Kin. Different anvils of gravity and radiation and evolution.

"If that winged creature is used to reading human minds, no wonder Marco's terrified it."

Marco's voice cut in, spiky with suspicion.

"What are you two talking privately about?"

"Female hygiene," said Silver crisply. "Marco, shouldn't we land again? We should interrogate this creature."

"I agree. I will watch for a suitable site. I am sorry to have interrupted your conversation." There was a click as he switched out.

There was a noise that might have been a shand chuckling. Then Silver said, "There is another minor matter, Kin. Are ravens a very common bird?"

"Hmm? I don't think so. Why?"

"There has been one in the sky ever since we left Eirick. Sometimes it merely tags behind, sometimes it flies a parallel course."

"It could be just coincidence," said Kin doubtfully.

"We've been flying at well over a hundred miles an hour at times, Kin."

"Good grief! You mean it's keeping up with us?"

"Yes. No, don't try and find it. It's well beyond human visual range, as it doubtless intends. It's only by accident I saw it once or twice, and then I started watching for it. At the moment I'm thinking in terms of a small flying robot."

"There was the raven in the ship," said Kin. "It got out of the box, remember? And before that it had arrived mysteriously at Kung Top. But we killed it in vacuum, didn't we?"

"I wonder if we did?"

They passed over a village where the only movement was in the flames of a burning house, and Marco cut in briefly to tell Kin to take Sphandor's tether while he went lower to investigate.

The demon hung a few meters away, wings pounding the air heavily. In the early-morning light Kin looked at him closely for the first time. She looked again. There was no doubt about it. He was fuzzy around the edges.

"I see it too," said Silver. "As if it's slightly out of focus. How odd."

Sphandor regarded them sullenly.

"YOU MEAN TO KILL ME," he whimpered.

"Not unless you attempt to do us harm," said Kin.

"THE SKINNY ONE, THE KALI-ARMED, HE WISHES TO KILL ME."

"That's just his general wish to the universe in general, not specific to you," said Kin. "I won't let him harm you."

"I WILL IMPLORE BERITH TO GIVE YOU GOLD! TRESOLAY I SHALL SUMMON TO MAKE YOUR BEAUTY EVEN MORE. . . ."

Marco was a dot on what, if it had been more than just a muddy open space, would have been called the village square.

"The place is empty," came his voice, "unless you count corpses."

They tethered Sphandor to a post in what had been the village forge. Kin touched his skin gingerly, and under her fingers the demon appeared to be vibrating like a wine-glass in a concert hall. Touching what looked like skin felt like fur, sticky with static.

A puzzle. She dozed off in the shade, watching Silver strip panels off the dumbwaiter and take the workshop manual from its drawer.

When she awoke the sun was high and 'waiter modules were stacked neatly in the dust. Silver was half-visible behind a pile of panels.

Through half-closed eyelids Kin watched Sphandor. He was hopping around anxiously on his tether, sometimes darting forward and passing a tool to the shand. When Silver's hand came out and groped in the air over a make-shift brazier for the soldering iron she'd made out of a piece of scrap copper, Sphandor reached into the coals and withdrew the rod by its glowing end, laying the other carefully in Silver's black palm.

"He just picked up a piece of red-hot iron," said Kin, "hot end first."

Silver looked at her blankly, then looked at Sphandor, then at the rod in her hand, then shrugged and turned back to the 'waiter's innards with a preoccupied air.

"It is a function of demons that they can withstand heat," came her muffled boice.

"How's the 'waiter?"

"Only superficial damage, but you know how it is—one has to remove half the machinery just to reach one wire. I've nearly finished."

Kin stood up, stretched, and wandered out into the square. She remembered something, and looked up at the sky.

"There is a raven perched on the big stone building over yonder," said Silver behind her.

"Do you think it's some sort of spy?"

"What do you think?"

"I think it's some sort of spy."

"That's what I think."

Kin turned around. "Where's Marco?" she asked. "It's time we interrogated wrinklebelly here."

"I PLEAD."

Silver slotted the last module into the dumbwaiter and started to clip the panels back before answering.

"He said he was going to have a look around. I told him about the raven."

Kin shook her head. "Not clever," she said. "Now he'll want to catch it. Sphandor could tell us more. About matter transmission, for one thing."

Silver glanced up sharply, then looked at the demon. He cringed. The shand walked over and stared at him, which made him attempt to shuffle behind the pole. Finally she took a magnifier out of the 'waiter tool kit and held it against his skin.

"Commendable reasoning," she said at last. "What gave you the idea, Kin?"

"He shouldn't be able to fly, even with chest muscles like that. And at that weight he should have legs like an elephant. And there's the fuzziness, of course, and the slight vibration."

Silver switched off the magnifier.

"I imagine the fuzziness is due to a malfunction in the transmitter," she said. "Well, well. It's a neat solution to the transmission problem, I'll give them that. Very neat. Frankly, Kin, you can stuff the disc. It's just a toy, a nasty toy. But this is something worth having."

"Right. Let's find Marco."

They found him inside the stone building that dominated

the village. At one end of it was a square tower, but he was standing like a statue in the gloom of the main hall. He turned as they came in, and in two of his hands were a pair of long candlesticks.

"What's this place?" asked Kin, staring up into the shadowy roof.

"A house of religion, I think," said the kung. "I was considering investigating the tower. There appears to be a stairway inside." He was unnaturally cheerful, and looked at her in an odd way.

"The view from the top should be extensive. We could plan the rest of the day's flight without putting a further drain on the belts' batteries."

"But the belts are perfectly—" Kin began, and stopped. Marco was semaphoring wildly with his two free arms.

"We must conserve our power!" Echoes bounced back from the depths of the building. He looked at Kin and pressed a finger to his lips for silence.

"Stay here, Silver," he said. "I want to show Kin this carving."

But when she went to step forward he pressed her back with one hand and walked away alone. He moved the two candlesticks expertly. It sounded as though two people were walking across the floor.

He's going really mad this time, Kin thought. Silver was smiling to herself.

Marco came back. "Now let's all go up the tower," he said. "This way, folks." He handed the sticks to Kin and pointed to the farther end of the hall, then soft-footed it toward the open door. They saw him flatten himself against the wall.

"Well, let's go," said Kin weakly, and started swinging the sticks. There was some difficulty in getting Silver up the winding staircase at the far end, and Kin felt a real fool helping two sticks to climb stairs.

"Learned something very interesting about the demon, Marco," said Silver. Then she replied in a remarkable impersonation of a kung: "What was that, Silver? Well, you know matter transmission has been tried and doesn't work? Well, it does on the disc. How do you mean? Kin noticed it. Tell him, Kin."

I'd better join in, she decided, otherwise they'll think I'm nuts. . . . What do I mean, *they*?

"The Company put a lot of research into straight matter transmission," she said. "In theory it ought to work; it's a logical extension of strata machine or dumbwaiter operation. Trouble is, it takes power. Far too much. And the best anyone managed was a two-millisecond displacement, then the subject just snapped back to the *here*."

"Aye, I heard about that," said Silver in Marco's voice. "The continuum is very anti sneaky stuff like matter transmission. Starhopping it has to put up with because we go through the Elsewhere, but straight teleportation is like trying to throw away a ball that's tied to your hand by elastic."

"Yes—there seems to be rules that say you stick to your predestined space-time point."

"What's that got to do with the demon?"

"He's transmitted. Something transmits him out maybe a hundred times a second, just as fast as the continuum snaps him back. That's how he can fly. They just move the focus of the transmitters. He's here, he can see and hear and touch but he's not *here*. I don't know why he stays tied up," she added as an afterthought. "They could move him outside the ropes."

"Then the sooner we get back—"

There was a scream.

Whey they arrived breathless at the doorway Marco was standing with all four hands clasped around a bundle of black feathers. Two small shining eyes watched them intently.

"It just sauntered in through the door," said the kung.

"What was all the business with the candlesticks?" said Kin. Silver snorted.

"Marco deduced the creature must have phenomenal sound detection apparatus," she said. "It seemed logical that if it heard three of us climbing the tower—"

"It's far too heavy for a bird," said Marco. "It must be a machine. Now we can talk to the disc controllers and explain—"

The raven turned its head one hundred and eighty degrees. Marco's mouth closed like a clam.

Quoth the raven: "You're the bastard that dumped me in vacuum. You're going to find out what happens to people who don't act respectful to one of the Eyes of God."

Marco's mouth opened and shut.

"Heaven help your hands if you're still holding me in five seconds," the bird added conversationally. "Four, three, two—" A thin wisp of smoke escaped from the feathers.

"Marco!"

His hands jerked back. The raven stayed in midair, balanced on a thin actinic flame that filled the hall with shadows and set the flagstone below cracking like spring-time ice.

Then it wasn't there. Kin had just enough sense to throw herself backward as pieces of roof rained down. They looked up at the ragged hole, far above, and heard the cry:

"You'll be sorreeee!"

"Talk," suggested Marco.

"I PLEAD."

"Who runs the disc? Where are they? How may we contact them? We shall require adequate directions and a detailed assessment of probable risks,"

Kin stepped forward and smiled reassuringly at the tethered giant. "Where did you come from, Sphandor?" she said.

"I HAVE ALWAYS UNDERSTOOD THAT A DOG WITH STOMACH GRIPES PAUSED NEAR A LOG AND THE SUN HATCHED ME OUT, LADY. DO NOT LET HIM NEAR ME! I CAN SEE HIS THOUGHTS AND—"

"I won't let him hurt you—"

"Oh yes? Just how?" Marco began angrily. Two of his hands were heavily bandaged.

"There is an island at the hub of the disc," said Kin sweetly, ignoring the interruption. "Tell me about it."

"GREAT LADY, GREAT BEASTS ROAM THERE OR SO IT IS SAID. NONE OF US MAY GO THERE ON PAIN OF—OF—"

"Of what?"

"AGONY, LADY. PAIN. THE WORLD DISAPPEARS, AND THEN ONE IS IN A NEW PLACE AND THERE IS AGONY."

"But you have attempted to go there?"

"THERE IS NOTHING THERE BUT BLACK SAND, LADY, AND THE BONES OF SHIPS, AND IN THE CENTER A DOME OF COPPER, AND TERRIBLE ENGINES! THEY CANNOT BE TRICKED!"

Kin kept trying for another ten minutes, then gave up.

"I believe him," she said, joining the others and dialing for coffee.

"He's manifestly a product of complex technology," said Marco.

"Yah, but he *thinks* he's a demon. What am I supposed to do? Argue?"

"If I chopped a foot off perhaps he would think differently? said Marco, reaching for a knife.

"No," said Silver, drumming her fingers on the dumbwaiter's dome. "No. I think not. Marco, we must assume that the disc builders tend to think like human beings, and humans set great store by mercy and fair play, at least when it does not conflict with their interests. Let us therefore set the creature free, thus demonstrating our moral superiority. The action will declare us to be merciful and civilized. In any case," she added, and they instinctively looked up for ravens as she lowered her voice, "I fail to see any further use in him."

Kin nodded. Silver walked and pulled at the knots in the cable and let it fall away. Sphandor stood up, looked at them solemnly, and walked out into the light.

He raised a cloud of dust as he took off, jerking upward like a man heron, and hovered fifteen meters up.

"ZAIGONEN TRYON (TFGKI) BERIGO HURSHIM!"

"So much for gratitude," said Silver.

"You understand the language?" said Kin.

"No, but I think I got the drift of that."

"ASFALAGO TEGERAM! NEMA! DWOLAH NARMA! WHERE ARE YOU, SOIGNATORIE, USORE, DILAPIDATOR—NOOOOOOOO—"

For an instant the demon was a black cloud that filled the sky, a fog of flickering, fuzzy images—each one staring in terror. Then he was gone. There was a *thump* of inrushing air.

They flew higher and fast over forests flattened by the falling ship. The smoke column was thinning, but now they were within miles of it the sky was all smoke.

Marco aimed directly at it, daring it to contain enemies. Ahead of Kin, his suit glittered like a silver spark against the darkness.

Once inside, Kin was surprised that she could still see. It might have been better if she could not. Between billows was the landscape of hell.

After five minutes inside the smoke Marco spoke.

"I don't understand it," he said. "There's no radiation

There *shouldn't* be. But there's far too much damage. Silver?"

Below them a drunken forest burned. Before the shand answered the ground below them disappeared abruptly, as if there had been a cliff.

"I can see nothing in this gloom," said Silver. "Can you?"

Marco could. Kung eyes had better night vision. He swore, and slowed his suit. The others did the same, drifting together so that the suits bobbed as in trio in the smoke. Marco was still staring down.

"I don't believe it," he said softly. "Let's go down."

"I'm flying blind," complained Silver. "You must direct me so that I don't hit the ground."

"You won't," said Marco.

Kin let herself drop, tensing herself for the crash until she came out of the smoke into moonlight.

Shining upward.

Vertigo gripped like a wrench. She could take space, because everywhere was down and direction lost its meaning. Skimming over a landscape was fine, it was no different than driving an aircar.

But not this. Not hanging legs down over a hole in the world.

The moon was directly below, hovering near infinity at the bottom of a tunnel that went down and down and down. . . .

"Five miles deep, wouldn't you agree, Silver?" said Marco in the distance. "And at least two wide. Are you all right, Kin?"

"Hunh?"

"You're still descending."

She fumbled dizzily for the suit controls. On a level with her eyes, a quarter mile away, was the lip of the hole, striated with bands of rock. Lower—she forced her eyes to move slowly. More bands, then a line of something metallic.

And a pipe, gushing water. Kin started to laugh hysterically.

"We're fine!" she giggled. "We don't need to go any farther, all we have to do is wait for the repairmen! You know what it's like with plumbers, when you want one they're never—"

"Cease gibbering. Silver, see to her," snapped Marco. Kin saw his hand poised over his chest panel. Then he dropped, fast. Her eyes started to follow him down before Silver's gloved paw jerked her around. She felt motion, and realized dimly that she was being steered away from the hole.

After a while she heard Marco say, "There's a pipe thirty meters across. Guess what? The water's pooling about two miles down—on air. That's why we're not in the middle of a descending hurricane—there's some kind of a gravity base down there. There's going to be one hell of a lake there soon.

"I've gone down forty meters. It looks like an explosion in a power station. There's sheared—cables, I guess, multicored—and what could be waveguide tubes or access tunnels or something. Silver?"

"I hear you. I suggest the ship impacted on top of one of the disc environmental machines, which blew up," said the shand.

"It looks like it. There's a lot of fused stuff and—scrub that. Here's a tunnel, a real tunnel. Can you hear me? I'm hovering in front of a semicircular tunnel, it's even got rails in it! The whole of the interior of the disc is one big machine! You should see this hole, it's big enough for a spaceship. There's uh, eighteen rails across the floor. Access for machinery repairs, I assume, but it's half choked with rubble."

"The ship impacted five days ago," said Silver somberly. "They have had five days in which to effect repairs. The disc builders are dead, Marco. There can be no other explanation."

"I can see no signs of repair," came the voice from the pit.

"Quite so. Something has gone wrong somewhere, just as the seas are erratic and the heavenly bodies misbehave. Which way does the tunnel run? Is there a continuation on the further side of the pit?"

There was a pause.

"Yes, I can see the other mouth of the tunnel. It runs direct from the rim to hub," said Marco. "I had considered suggesting we continue our flight along the tunnel but—"

"—it would be better to face any dangers in the open sky. Precisely."

Kin opened her eyes. She was hovering over blessed earth—scorched, maybe, baked and half molten, but solid

"Thanks," she said. "Stupid, wasn't it? My forebears used to hang from trees by their knees."

"No shame," said Silver. "I do not like darkness. We all have our phobias. Kin? You look a little pale. . . ."

Kin didn't try to speak. She knew she couldn't. She managed a strangled grunt, and pointed.

Something was rising out of the pit, with difficulty. That difficulty arose because it was almost too big. All she could think of was the Mt. Tryggvason Memorial.

It was one of the Valhallian tourist attractions. Someone had carved the high-relief heads of President Halfdan, Thorbjorn, Weasel Moccasin and Teuhtlile out of solid rock a few hundred feet high in the side of the mountain.

That was what was rising out of the pit—a Mt. Tryggvason with one head missing, a three-headed Thing. Only the head facing them was human. The others could have been a monstrous toad and some sort of insect, giant faces merging sickeningly into an impossible head, and atop the head were three crowns big enough for houses. Below the heads a cluster of spider legs dangled, each one a hundred meters long.

The effect was slightly marred by the fact that the far side of the pit could be seen through the image.

"Marco," said Silver.

"I don't think there's any more to be learned down—"

"Did anything pass you on the way up?"

"I don't understand."

"Look up, Marco."

"Holy shit!"

Kin choked.

"Do not be afraid," said Silver reassuringly.

"Afraid of that?" said Kin. "That monstrosity? I'm just ood and angry, Silver. Know what that thing is? A comic carecrow, an image sent out to scare away anyone who iight look into the pit and find out about the disc.

"If we get back I won't care who built the disc, I'll see at they're broken. Busted. Bankrupted. They've built a orld people sail off the edge of, and get chased by demons nd are superstitious because that's how you survive! I'm eginning to hate it!"

Marco rose like a rocket in the center of the image, ecame a glitter in the eye of Saitan, a spark in the brain f God.

"Intangible," he reported. "A mere image."

The great human face, kingly and cold, twisted. The mouth opened, and the pit echoed to a great sad sigh. And a lightning bolt struck out of the smoking sky and melted the dumbwaiter so thoroughly that droplets of hot metal spilled toward the bright obversical sky.

Hail drummed off Kin's suit. They were flying now against a deadline.

In fifty hours, or less, Silver would go mad and attempt suicide. Kung and men could go for a long time without food. Shandi could not.

The storm raged all around them, but sank away as Marco led them upward. They burst out of the clouds into a disc sunset.

It was far behind them, red and angry and barred with cloud. Judging from the sky the whole of the disc was having bad weather, and bad wasn't really the word. Some of those cloud shapes were mad.

Marco broke the silence. "We have a thousand miles to cover," he said.

"That gives us an average speed of twenty miles an hour," said Kin. "We could easily reach the hub, even with a few rest stops."

"So we reach the hub. Do we find a dumbwaiter there?"

"Anyone capable of building the disc could build a dumbwaiter."

"Why didn't they repair the hole, then? Eirick, Lothar—they are descendants of your disc builders, reverted to savagery. Or the disc builders are dead."

"Okay, have you got any better ideas?"

Marco snorted.

Silver was trailing half a mile behind them, a dot against the livid sky. She rumbled politely to show that she was in circuit.

"There is a possibility we may find a 'waiter," she said "if the disc was built by the Company. Don't groan, Kin. In many ways the idea of the disc would fit in with the Policy.

"By the way, there is a raven flying half a mile behind me."

Kin stared at the rushing clouds below. Policy. Perhaps the disc was Policy. . . .

* * *

The Great Spindle Kings, Wheelers, paleotechs, ChThones—people of the universe. The universe *was* people.

Once upon a time astrohistorians had thought in terms of a vast, empty starry stage, a blank canvas waiting for the brush of life. In fact it was now understood that Life of a kind had appeared within three microseconds of the monobloc's explosion. If it hadn't, the universe would now be randomized matter. It was Life which had directed its growth. Life had once resided in the vast spinning dust clouds that became stars—every star was the skeleton of one of the great dust-accreting dinosaurs of the universe's Jurassic.

Later lifeforms had been smaller, brighter. Some, like the Wheelers, had been evolutionary dead ends. Some, notably the Great Spindle Kings and the shameleons, had been successful in the only way that evolution measured success—they survived longer. But even star-striding races died. The universe was tombs upon graves upon mausoleums. The comet that brightened the pagan skies was the abraded corpse of a scientist, three eons ago.

The Policy of the Company was simple. It was: Make Man immortal.

It would take a while, and had only just started. But if Man could be spread thinly on many different planets, so that he became many types of Man, perhaps he would survive. The Spindles had died because they were so alike. Now, upon dozens of worlds, men were being changed by different forces, maddened by different moons, bent by different gravities.

Since the universe could not be said to have a natural ending, because the universe was not natural but only the sum of the lives that had shaped it, Men intended to live forever. Why not?

Preserve meme pools, preserve ideas, that was the secret. If you had a hundred planets there was room for different sciences, curious beliefs, new techniques, old religions to flourish in quiet corners. Earth had been one united civilization and had nearly perished once because of it. Diversify enough, and somewhere you'll always find someone capable of catching anything the future throws at you.

People on a disc guarded by demons and ringed with a waterfall—what memes would they contribute to the genetics of civilization? She tried to explain to Marco.

"What are memes?" said Marco.

"Meme are—ideas, attitudes, concepts, techniques," said Kin. "Mental genes. Trouble is, all the memes likely to develop on the disc are host-destructive. Anthropocentricity is one."

A pale-red moon rose above the curdled clouds. Now they flew a mile apart, flew high and fast to make the hours count. Kin kept an eye on the speck that was Silver, and worried.

Quite wrong, of course, to project human thought patterns on an alien, but a man in Silver's position would live in hope that sooner or later food would be forthcoming. Men were optimists.

You couldn't expect a shand to think like a man. It was so easy to think of your friends as humans in a skin, and for good and noble reasons people were encouraged to think of aliens as funny-shaped men. Just because they learned to play poker or read Latin didn't make them human.

In short, Kin wondered when Silver would attempt suicide. She signaled Marco and told him.

"We can do nothing," he said. "I have already decided to eat no food until we reach the hub, as a gesture of solidarity. We could take disc proteins, if the 'waiter's analysis was right," he added.

"Will that make her feel better?"

"It may make *us* feel better. However, there is another problem that has recently forced itself on my attention. I hesitate to mention it—"

"Mention it, mention it."

"Look at the panel on your left wrist. There's an orange fluorescent line against a green strip. See it?"

Kin squinted down in the flickering light.

"I see it. Only it's an orange dot."

"Quite, but it should be a line. We really are running out of gas, Kin."

They flew in silence for a while. Then Kin asked, "How long?"

"About six hours for you and me. Perhaps an hour less for Silver. That will solve one problem. She'll come to earth miles behind us."

"Except that we will of course stay with her," said Kin flatly. Marco appeared not to have heard.

"If we still had the 'waiter the problem would not have been insurmountable. The hub is not too far. We could have terrorized disc people into transporting us. A hundred suggestions leap to the mind. It might have been quite enjoyable, and good experience."

"Experience for what?"

"Hobnobbing with the disc folk on a superior basis. I had planned, should the hub hold nothing of interest, to set up an empire. Surely the idea had occurred to you?"

It had, in passing. Kin thought for a while of Genghis Marco, Marco Caesar, Prester Marco. He could do it, at that. A four-armed god king.

"How long would you say it would take the disc to get onto a spacegoing footing?" he asked. "If that was made a goal, I mean? We have the knowledge."

"No, we don't. We *think* we do, but all we know is how to operate machines. Of course, you could get a spaceship built inside a decade."

"That soon? Then we could—"

"No we couldn't." Kin had been thinking about this, too. "What could be built is a primitive capsule powered by solid-fuel rockets with enough oomph to ram the outer dome. You could launch it by dropping it over the waterfall."

"First we'd have to unify the disc," said Marco thoughtfully. "Not difficult. Give me five hundred Norsemen and—"

"There's Silver," said Kin. "And anyway, I have great hopes of the hub."

Even so . . .

She had been doing a lot of thinking, before they lost the 'waiter. With the 'waiter they might have conquered the disc, filled the void left by the presumably departed disc creators. Without it, the best they could hope for was a comfortable life. In a strange way it wouldn't be so bad for the other two. They would be aliens, marooned on a strange world. *She* would be marooned among people. It was possible that she had more in common with Silver and Marco than she did with the barbarians down there. It was a dreadful possibility.

"These belts are supposed to be able to fly you halfway across a system and land you on a planet," she complained.

"They were not expected to carry people thousands of miles against gravity, including many changes of altitude," said Marco. "It is most vexing."

"Vexing!"

"If you feel so strongly, I suggest you make a complaint to the manufacturers."

"How can—was that a joke?" said Kin. "Good grief!"

Dawn saw them flying over semidesert and scrub, in a sky free of clouds. Once they passed over a camel train, almost invisible were it not for its skeletal, juddering shadow on the sand.

They had drifted slightly off their course during the night, and as far as Marco could estimate were speeding down the Tigris-Euphrates valley.

"That puts us in southeast Turkey," said Marco, and added wistfully, "That means Baghdad. I should like to have seen Baghdad."

"Why?" said Kin.

"Oh, when I was a kid my foster-folks bought me a book of fantasy stories about, well, genies and magic lamps and such. It made a big impression on me."

"Don't suggest landing," said Kin. "Don't even *think* about it."

But they passed over a city of low white houses surrounding palaces and strangely domed buildings. A tent town lay outside the walls. The river the city straddled was noticeably a different color downstream, and low enough between its banks to speak of drought. Now the sun was well up the ground shimmered.

A mile later Silver's belt failed. There was no question of a crash—instead all forward power ceased as the batteries' waning ergs buoyed her gently to the ground.

The others followed her down into a grove of knotted, sweet-smelling trees. When Kin took off her helmet the heat hit her like the breath of Hell. *Too* hot, she decided. No wonder the fields looked scorched. From here the river was a blood-colored snake winding weakly between slabs of cracked mud.

"Well," she said vaguely. She meant This Is It.

"I am at a loss," said Marco, moving hurriedly into the heady shade under the trees.

"You mean you don't have a plan?"

"Your meaning?"

"Oh, forget it." Kin took a sip of water from the suit's reservoir. Have to be careful about that, too.

Silver sat with her back against a trunk, staring vaguely at the city. Behind her the sun was a copper rivet in a sky like hot iron.

Then she commented. "An aircraft has just risen."

He was old in looks at least, his face wrinkled like an old apple. His gray beard was intricately styled. His eyes seemed to show neither whites nor expression. Certainly he did not seem surprised.

Disc builder? While Kin watched him and Silver talking, facing each other cross-legged under the trees, she thought hard and fast. His clothing didn't look anything but barbarously splendid, but she was no arbiter of disc fashion. His craft was technologically advanced, and he knew how to use it—at the moment it was folded up inside a pouch on the belt of his traveling companion, a large broad man wearing nothing but a loincloth and a dour expression. He held a long curved sword, and his eyes never left Marco.

Kin slid across to the kung.

"I wonder where he keeps his antipersonnel blaster," she asked. "Marco, you know you and Silver had this idea about how I could survive on the disc by using sex?"

"You have that advantage, yes."

"Well, forget it."

"Your meaning?"

"Just forget it. Our fat friend with the sword is—" she stopped, furious to feel herself reddening. "Marco, can't you recall *anything* else from that storybook?"

Marco's face was blank for a while. Then he winced. "Ah yes," he said. "You mean, like, *unique*."

"Not too unique for this time and place," said Kin, and turned toward Silver. The shand looked up at her.

"This could be Arabic," she said. "I've never heard it spoken. I've tried a bit of Latin, which I think he understands but he's not letting on. The only thing I've established so far is that he wants our suits."

Kin and Marco exchanged glances. A look of almost Ehftnic guile spread across the kung's face.

"Tell him they're very precious," he said. "Tell him we wouldn't exchange them even for his aircraft. Tell him we need to get to the coast quickly."

"He'll never fall for that," said Kin. "Anyway, there's hardly any juice left in the belts."

"That's his worry," said Marco. "I have a plan. But first of all I'd like to see how he operates that flying rug. Tell him it is too hot to negotiate out here—it's true, anyway."

There followed a long exchange of cracked phrases and words repeated at varying levels of exasperation. Finally the man nodded and stood up, motioning toward the servant with a hand.

The big man stepped forward and reached into his pouch, handing his master the—call it the—

Hell, thought Kin, it *is* a flying carpet. Only we don't like to say it because it sounds crazy.

It was about two meters by three, and patterned with an intricate geometrical design in blue, green and red. Spread out on the ground it hugged the bumps and hollows limply.

The man said a word. Some dust was blown up as the carpet straightened, stiffened and hovered a few inches above the sand; Kin thought she could hear a faint hum.

It didn't rock even when Silver stepped aboard. The man with the sword sat beside them. The old man said another word. The ground fell away noiselessly.

"One could coat a surface with flexible lifting units," said Marco after a while, with a brave little quiver in his voice, "but what about power? How could you get batteries this thin?"

Similar thoughts had been passing through Kin's mind, since she was staring intently at the carpet between her knees so that her eyes didn't stray over the edge. She was aware that Marco was sliding gingerly toward her.

"You nervous too?" she said.

"I am conscious of mere millimeters of unknown and unproven flying machine underneath me," he said.

"You weren't nervous in the lift belts."

"But they were under an unconditional hundred-year-guarantee. If one belt failed, how long would the manufacturer stay in business?"

"I do not think one could fall off this if one tried," said Silver. She hit the air beside her with a paw and it made a noise, as though someone had punched a jelly.

"Safety field," she said. "Try it."

Kin waved a hand gingerly over the carpet's edge. It was like moving through treacle and, as she pushed, like leaning on rock. Ali Baba turned round, grinned at her and spoke a sentence.

When the carpet was finally flying level again there was silence. Finally Marco said flatly: "Tell the lunatic if he attempts that again I will kill him."

Kin released her numb fingers from their grip on the patterned pile.

"Be diplomatic," she added. "Be tactful. Say that if he does it again I will maim him."

Two loops and a triple roll!

On the disc-generated gravity, shaped fields and direct vocal control came wrapped up in one neat carpet-shaped vehicle.

She wondered how Marco intended to steal it.

They skimmed low over the flat roofs of the city. Kin saw people in the narrow crowded streets look up, then turn back and go about their business. Magic carpets, apparently, were familiar objects.

They homed in on a minor palace, a squat white affair with a central dome and two ornate towers. There was a garden behind decorative trellises—now, that was odd. . . .

"It must have its own source of water," she said aloud.

"Why?" said Marco.

"Everything else around here is parched. That's the one green spot we've seen today."

"That would not be surprising, if he is a disc builder," said Marco. "A fact which I doubt."

"And I also," rumbled Silver, "yet he handles the carpet well enough and our flying belts evinced only cautious greed, not awe. I am thinking now in terms of some hermetic order, maybe, handing down disc-builder machines and relics with no proper understanding of their internal workings—as a savage may competently drive a groundcar while believing it to be powered by little horses under the engine cowling."

Ali Baba brought them down perfectly, the carpet drifting slowly across a balcony and through an arch into a high-ceilinged room. It hovered a few inches above the intricately tiled floor, then settled.

He leaped up and clapped his hands. By the time the others had untwisted their limbs and, in Marco's case, eased the steel grip his hands had been maintaining, a posse of servants had entered the room. They carried towels, and wide bowls.

"That'd better be water," growled Marco, " 'cause I'm gonna drink it."

He pushed his head noisily into the bowl in front of him, causing mild consternation among the servants. Silver picked up hers and, after a preliminary sniff, opened her mouth like a funnel and tipped it down. Kin drank her fill in a reasonably ladylike manner, and used the rest to wash the dust off her face.

She took the opportunity to look around.

There was hardly any furniture. The room was just an ornate box, wall decorated with geometrical and horticultural patterns and several large screens at one end. By the grounded carpet was a low table, its top apparently one thick slab of crystal.

Ali had disappeared, along with the servants. Silver peered around the room.

"The water was ice-cold," she stated. "There were crystals in it. Show me iced water, and I'll show you civilization."

"Anywhere else it would mean a refrigerator," Kin admitted, "but here, I'd bet they've got hot-and-cold running demons in all rooms."

Marco walked over to the carpet and inspected it carefully. Then he stepped on it and said the word.

"I imagine it's slaved to his voice pattern," said Silver, without looking around. Marco cursed quietly.

Ali Baba appeared from behind the screens, followed by two men with swords. He was carrying a small black box on a red cushion.

He looked sideways at Silver and spoke a few words in halting Latin.

"He is going to, uh, summon that-which-speaks-all-tongues," she said. "I think."

While they watched he laid the box on the floor and opened the lid. The thing he took out puzzled Kin. It looked like a small flat teapot made out of adulterated gold.

He polished it with his sleeve.

"Will You Give Me No Peace, Sorcerer?"

IT had appeared a few feet away, hazy in a cloud of purple smoke. It was immediately obvious to Kin why Marco's appearance hadn't bothered the man—if he was used to things that looked like this, he was used to *anything*.

It was man-height, or would have been if it stood erect. But it was bent almost double, two thick gold-scaled arms and oversized hands serving as a second pair of legs. Clusters of tendrils grew out of its neck. Its face was long, vaguely horselike, topped by a pair of pointy ears and tailed by two mustachios that trailed on to the floor. It wore a small cone-shaped hat.

"Know All That I Am Azrifel," it began in a singsong voice, "Djinnee of the Desert, Terror of Thousands, Scourge of Millions, and, I Must Be Frank About It, Slave of the Lamp. So What Do You Want This Time, Master?"

There was a long speech from the sorcerer. The djinnee turned around until it faced the trio.

"My Master Abu Ibn Infra Presents His Compliments And Welcomes You to His Humble Abode and a Lot of Stuff Like That. If You Want to Eat, Just Tell the Table. Your Wish Is Its Command. There's a Lot of That Sort of Thing Goes On Around Here," he added.

Kin hunkered down beside the table and looked at it more closely. It was one block of crystal, but now that she paid close attention there seemed to be something else in there too, something like a moving wisp of faint smoke.

She thought of cucumber and green paprillion salad, and the cinnamon ice cream she used to buy from Grnh's Olde Drugge Store in Wonderstrands, the one with the recipe that Grnh had refused to sell to the dumbwaiter programmers. There was always a black Treale cherry on the top. The memory of that taste welled up until she drooled.

It grew out of the table. There was an impression of swirling movement in the crystal and then it was there, smoking with frost.

There was a black Treale cherry on the top. And—Kin picked up the carton and stared.

It was in a familiar blue, black and white and showed an anthropomorphic penguin in a chef's hat. Around the side was: "The Olde Drugge Store, corner of Skrale and High, Upperside, Wonderstrands 667548. Tregin Grnh and Siblings, reg. WE FREEZE TO PLEASE."

Marco stared at the carton, then looked down at the teasing shadows in the tabletop.

"I don't know how you managed that," he said carefully, "but what I have in mind is the Blue Plate special they serve in Henry Horse's Kung Food Bar in New—"

He stopped, because it was already there. There was

one bowl, heavy pottery containing something under an orange-yellow crust that rumbled with internal eruptions.

"It must use telepathy," he said uncertainly. "It's just a telepathic dumbwaiter. Come on, Silver. I'm hungry."

"*You're* hungry," said Silver. She drummed heavy fingers on the table edge, then doubtfully:

"I have in mind a dish of ceremonial truduc."

The shadow swirled, disappeared. Silver's fingers drummed on.

"Smoked guaracuc with grintzes?" she suggested.

A vague shape appeared above the crystal, then faded.

"Dadugs in Brine? Chaque sweetbreads? Xiqua? Dried qumqums?"

Kin sighed, and pushed the ice cream away untasted.

"There Is a Problem?" said Azrifel.

"The table can't handle Shand proteins," said Silver, sitting down heavily and drawing her knees up to her chin.

"What Is a Protein?"

Abu Ibn Infra seated himself comfortably by the far side of the table and put out his hand to grasp a crystal glass of pinkish liquid as it materialized beside him. Azrifel stirred, and nodded as the man spoke.

"My Master Wishes to Talk About Your Flying Clothes and Similar Matters." More consultation. "My Master Presents His Compliments to His Fellow Collectors and Offers, In Exchange for All Three Items, a Mirror-to-See-All-Things-Be-They-Never-So-Far and Two Bottomless Purses."

Kin was aware of the other two looking at her. She said, "Leaving aside for a moment his somewhat derisory offer"—she had a feeling that a lack of the haggling spirit might be regarded as signs of general weakness—"we come from a far-off land and do not quite understand the reference to collectors. Collectors of what?"

Abu Ibn Infra frowned as he listened to the translation. He spat out a reply. Kin wouldn't have thought it possible for anyone to spit several lengthy sentences, but he managed, he managed.

"My Master Is Puzzled. You Possess Gifts of God but You Do Not Know of the Collectors. He Says: How Can This Be?"

"Listen, demon," said Kin, "*you* know. You're a projection, like Sphandor. Aren't you?"

"I Find Myself Forbidden to Answer That Question at

This Moment in Time," said Azrifel smugly. "You Are in the Shit, That's All I Know. If You Think You're Coming Out of This Alive, My Reaction Is Ho Ho Ho."

"I will kill it," said Marco, half rising. The guards behind Ibn Infra stirred.

"Sit down," hissed Kin. "You, demon, answer the question. What is a collector?"

"My Master Says It Is No Secret. He Himself Was Once a Humble Fisherman Until, Upon Gutting a Fish, One Day, He Discovered Inside It a Gift of God, to Wit, the Lamp to Which I Am Shamefully Enslaved. I Am Azrifel of the Ninth Dominion of the Damned. I Can Find Anything—Even the Power to Talk to You. That Is My Power.

"For Five Years I have Labored Mightily for This Jumped-Up Pig of a Nouveau Riche Former Fisherman, Spiriting to This Somewhat Pretentious Palace Such Gifts of God as Are Unclaimed by Other Collectors or in the Possession of Collectors Unfortunate Enough to Have Demons Weaker Than I. I Have Combed the Depths of the Sea and the Bowels of Volcanoes, I Have—"

"Hold it," said Kin. "The flying carpet, the table, these damn money purses—they're Gifts of God?"

"Aye. The Carpet I Liberated from a Merchant in Basra, The Table I Found Encrusted with Barnacles on the Sea Floor—"

"But your master doesn't know how they operate? I mean, they're just magical items to him?"

"Aren't They, Then?" said the demon, grinningly.

"Just as I thought," snapped Marco. "He's just an ignorant man who doesn't know any more about the nature of the disc than does anyone else in these parts. I'll take out these guards, then we'll grab him and ride the carpet out of here."

"Wait a minute," said Kin sharply.

"What for? He knows nothing except how to operate the toys this creature finds for him."

Kin shook her head. "Just once, let's try diplomacy," she said. "Demon, tell your master we are not collectors. We will give him these flying belts for his collection if he transports us on his magic carpet to the circular island that lies off the coast to the southeast of here."

She knew she had said something wrong as soon as the

words were out of her mouth. When Azrifel's translation died away Abu's face went white.

Marco sighed, and stood up. "Okay, so much for diplomacy," he said. He sprang. So did Azrifel. There was a gray-and-yellow blur in midair and a small thunderclap. Then the demon was back, unruffled. Marco had vanished.

"What have you done with him?" said Kin.

"He Has Been Deposited in a Place of Safety, Unharmed Except Maybe for a Few Friction Burns."

"I see. And his ransom is our flying belts, right?"

Abu spoke. The demon said: "No, My Master Says He Knows Now That You Come from Another World. There Was Another Such Traveler, Some Time Since, Who—"

"Jago Jalo?" said Kin. Abu glared at her.

"Crazy fool," hissed Silver.

"That Was His Name," agreed the demon. "A Madman. He Abused Our Hospitality. He Stole from Our Collection. He Sought the Forbidden Island Too."

"What happened to him?" said Kin. The demon shrugged.

"He Escaped from Here with a Carpet, a Bottomless Purse and a Cloak with Unusual Powers. Even I Have Been Unable to Locate Him. My Master Feels, However, That All Is Not Lost."

"No?"

"He Has Three New Flying Devices, Two Captive Demons and You."

Kin sprang around. More guards had appeared on the balcony, and they were archers. She considered taking a dive for the open air with the belt on full throttle. She might get hit. She doubted whether the disc's medical facilities were satisfactory. Anyway, that wouldn't solve Silver's problem.

So she collapsed into tears of inconsolable grief.

She heard a brief conversation between the demon and his master. Then two servant women were summoned to take her away.

She had one glimpse of Silver's impassive face before she was escorted out of the room and into a maze of ornate arches and screens. A male guard walked behind her with a drawn sword.

The women chattered at her solicitously. When they reached one arched doorway the guard left them, and took up a post outside the door. Kin was briefly surrounded by a gaggle of small dark-eyed women in scanty clothing before the older of her escorts shooed them away. She felt helpful arms guiding her to a bench. She sat and stared.

Later a middle-aged woman brought her some food. Kin looked up at her gratefully. Under the strange makeup the woman was watching her with simpleminded sympathy.

So Kin apologized silently as she hit her, as nicely as possible. The woman sighed and collapsed, but Kin was already on her feet and running.

She sped through several low and airy rooms and had a blurred impression of fountains, singing birds and bored women sitting on large cushions. Kohl-eyed, they stared after her and began to scream as Kin cannoned into a servant carrying a tray.

A long way behind her a new series of screams suggested that a guard had reluctantly invaded the seraglio.

Kin reached a balcony, considered the courtyard below, then scrambled up a decorative trellis that trembled even under her weight. It took her onto a flat roof and into the full glare of the noon sun.

Shouts below meant that a guard had got as far as the balcony. Kin threw herself down, chest heaving, hoping that he would think she had taken the easy way and dropped into the courtyard. He didn't. There was a sudden silence, broken by some heavy breathing.

Then wood cracked, and there was the beginning of a wail that ended with a noise like a falling man hitting hard stone flags.

She jogged across the roof to the nearer of two towers that pierced it. It wasn't a wise choice really, but she couldn't think of anything else. There was an arch with no door, and a dark spiral stairway as cold as ice after the glare of the sun off the roof.

The stairs ended in a turret room with glassless windows looking out over the city. Kin peered around in the gloom. It looked as if she was in a storeroom.

There were a few carpets rolled up against the wall, and boxes in untidy heaps beside them. A tall bronze statue in vaguely Middlesea dress was propped against a three-legged table with what looked like the wreckage of a drinking party strewn across it. There were several swords, including one that looked—Kin couldn't believe it, but closer inspection bore out the first impression—one that *was* half buried in an anvil.

In the middle of the floor was a statue of a horse, cast in some dark metal. The musculature had been done well, but the pose was uninspiring. It just stood foursquare, looking at the floor.

"Junk," said Kin. She tried to pull an iron-bound chest across the stair hole, then gave up and sat on it instead. There was no sound below.

A person could hold out here for weeks, she thought. "With food and water, that is." Food! She thought longingly of the magic table, or even of the dumbwaiter. But she couldn't have eaten a meal with Silver watching her sorrowfully, knowing that inside two days the shand would turn despite herself into a ravening, ravenous animal.

"Marco? Silver?" she whispered.

At the fifth attempt Marco answered.

"Kin! Where are you?"

"I'm up in—is there anyone with you?"

"We're in a zoo! You wouldn't believe it! You must get us out!"

"I'm in some sort of museum attic," she said. "I'll have to wait until it's dark. Where are you exactly?"

"I assume we're somewhere in the palace grounds. You must work quickly. *Silver and I are in the same cage.*"

"What's she doing now?"

"Moping."

"Oh-oh."

"What?"

Kin sighed. "I'll do my best," she said. She padded over to a window and peered out. Someone was shouting in the distance, but the roof lay hot and empty below her. There was, she noticed, a black speck wheeling in the sky. One of the Eyes of God, whoever He was.

Most of the swords she could hardly lift with both hands, so they were out.

"Let's face it," she told herself, "how are you going to make the big heroic rescue in any case?"

On the other hand, she answered, it'll be expected of you. The races of the galaxy look toward mankind as the essential lunatic element.

She stepped backward, and knocked against the table. The jug on it fell over, and spilled vinegar-smelling wine across the table and onto the floor in a thin stream. Kin watched it for a while, then carefully set the jug upright.

It swished.

Looking inside, she saw dark liquid rising. She waiting until the jug was brim-full of swirling redness, then grabbed the handle, sloshed the liquid across the room and brought the base of the jug down hard against the tabletop.

There was a sizzle and a brief smell of ozone. Bits of circuit laminate bounced on the floor.

"Fine," she said softly, "that's just fine. So long as it wasn't the fairies that were doing it." On the other hand, the Company didn't believe in matter transmission either. But it might have been, say, a tiny single-function dumb-waiter in the base of the jug, sucking up molecules from the ambient air. She decided she'd believe anything but magic.

Someone moved, down at the base of the staircase.

There was nowhere to hide. Correction—the tower room was bursting with hiding places, but none of them promised to be permanent. Kin grabbed a sword from a pile nearby and considered hacking at the first head to appear on the stairs.

No good. She looked up at a small trapdoor in the ceiling, and decided it would be easier to defend. If it led onto the roof, perhaps the raven would see her—as if that would do any good. Anyway, she could then slice at fingers.

She walked over to the horse statue and hoisted herself into a stirrup, then stood up on tiptoe in the saddle to fumble with the trapdoor.

The horse whirred. Kin swayed, landed sitting in the saddle but with enough force to knock the breath out of her. Then she couldn't move her legs. She looked down in panic. Padded clamps had extruded from the horse's flanks and were gripping her gently but firmly.

The neck in front of her came up. The head swiveled one hundred and eighty degrees and the horse looked at Kin with bright insectile eyes.

"YOUR WISH IS MY COMMAND," it said inside Kin's head.

"Hell!"

"THOSE ARE NOT MEANINGFUL COORDINATES."

"Are you a robot?"

She felt the click and whirr of gears underneath her.

"I AM THE FABULOUS MECHANICAL HORSE OF AHMED, PRINCE OF TREBISOND."

Kin heard scurrying footsteps on the stairs.

"Get me out of here!" she hissed.

"PLEASE HOLD ON TO THE REINS. PLEASE LOWER THE HEAD. IN CASE OF MALAISE OF THE AIR, PLEASE USE THE RECEPTACLE PROVIDED."

There was a *thud* inside the animal, and the noise of heavy wheels tumbling into motion. The horse took off. As they glided smoothly through the window Kin flung herself forward to avoid the edge of the wall. And then the horse was free and moving, legs galloping on the air as it soared into the copper sky.

Kin looked at the sword in her hand. It was night-black and unnaturally light, but it would do. It would be surprising if Abu had learned how to use the lift belts yet, so possibly his only other aircraft was the carpet.

If it came to an aerial fight, she'd prefer to be on the horse.

"YOUR FURTHER WISH IS MY COMMAND."

"You can start by telling me how you fly," said Kin, peering at the gardens below.

"ABANAZZARD THE MAGICIAN FABRICATED ME. I FLY BY APPLICATION OF THE COMPOUND UPSWINGING WEIGHT ENGINE, WHICH REQUIRES THE CONTINUED INTERVENTION OF THE DJINNEE ZOLAH AT THE CRITICAL POINT."

"Do you know of a zoo in the palace grounds?"

"YES."

"Land inside it, then."

"TO HEAR IS TO OBEY, O MISTRESS."

The horse started to gallop in a descending spiral. Kin was briefly aware of upturned faces as they raced at roof height back toward the palace. A ragged line of dusty trees flashed past and Kin realized they were landing in a wide avenue between rows of low cages, dark and forbidding in the gathering dusk.

Her mount touched down neatly, hooves galloping smoothly from empty air to packed earth. Something hurled itself against the bars of the nearest cage, and she got a vague impression of wings and teeth. Plenty of teeth.

"Marco!" Things shrilled and sneezed in the shadows of the cages.

"Over here!"

Kin urged the horse forward until she saw Marco's gleaming eyes looking urgently between bars thick enough to have been tree trunks. Perhaps they were.

Kin jiggled them until they slid back noisily. Marco came out as though on a spring.

"Give me the sword," he commanded. Kin had almost handed it over before it occurred to her that she could have refused, and then it was too late. He snatched it.

"Is this the best you could do?" he hissed. "It's blunt as a ball."

"Big deal! I could have gone off and left you!"

Marco tapped the flat of the black sword on one opened palm, and looked at her reflectively.

"Yes," he said. "You could. This sword will do. Thank you. From where did you obtain the flying robot?"

"Well, I went—"

"How do you make it fly?"

"It just obeys, and—*get down*!"

Marco settled himself in the saddle, and ignored her.

"Do you know the way to the palace, robot quadruped?"

"YES, O MASTER."

"Then proceed."

There was a brief drumming of hooves and the horse was a dwindling speck against the sky. Kin watched it disappear and then peered into the back of the cage.

"Silver?" she said quietly. A light shape stirred in the gloom.

"Come on," said Kin. "We'd better be going. How do you feel?"

Silver sat up.

"Where is the kung?" she said thickly.

"Gone to beat up the baddies, the lunatic fool."

"Then where should *we* go?" said the shand, lumbering to her feet.

"After him, I think. Got any better ideas?"

"No," said Silver. "I imagine everyone will be far too occupied to notice us."

They stepped out into the avenue of bars.

"There are unicorns in that one," volunteered Silver, pointing. "We saw them being fed. And mermaids. I think, in a pool. They were given fish."

"Abu is a born collector, it seems."

They passed a white dome, temple-size. Close up, it was

a large white egg, the lower third buried in the sand. There was a small hole in one end.

"Laid by a bird?" said Silver, indicating it with a thumb.

"Search me. I wouldn't put out crumbs for it. There's another one over there. No—"

It wasn't. It was, however, the derelict shell of the planetary lander from a Terminus probe. A memory arose in Kin unbidden, of an ancient copy of a still more ancient publicity film. It looked smaller in real life. There were three deep gashes in it, as though some great beast had tried to grab it.

Perhaps it had. If the thing beside it was an egg, *something* laid it.

The interior was a mess.

"Jalo landed near the center of the disc, at least," said Silver. Kin looked at the—oh, all right, call them talon marks—they could have been.

"I don't envy him," she said. "Our Abu is a genuine enthusiast, Silver. He never throws anything away."

There were running feet behind them, and they turned to see two men gaping at them. One held a pike, and prodded it gingerly toward Silver. It was a mistake. The shand merely grabbed it behind the point and felled its holder with a vicious downward slash, bringing it back afterward to knock the other man's scurrying legs from under him.

Then she started running toward the palace, wielding the shattered shaft like a club.

Kin trailed after her. There didn't seem any alternative.

They found Marco by following the screams.

There was a courtyard, and a mob of fighting men, and in the middle a blur behind a fence of swords. Marco was fighting five men at once, and seemed to be winning.

One man, who turned and found himself a few feet from Silver, slashed at her with desperate bravery. She blinked at him sleepily, then brought a fist down with vertebra-crushing speed.

And all the time the sword sang. Kin had heard the phrase used poetically, but this one *was* singing—a weird electric ululation punctuated by clashes and screams.

Marco was holding it at arm's length, almost cringing away from it. It moved of itself, darting from blade to blade, from blade to body, without appearing to pass through the intervening air. Blue light crackled along its edge.

Silver padded up to two men and hit them hard. Of the ones who turned to stare before running away, three keeled over as Marco took advantage of their distraction.

Alone in the courtyard, except for the dead, Marco sagged and dropped the sword. Kin picked it up and looked at its edge. It should have been bloody. It wasn't. It was merely black, like a hole through the universe into something else.

"It's alive," said Marco sullenly. "I know you will scorn, but—"

"What we have here," said Kin loudly, "is merely a frictionless-coated blade with an electronic edge. The metal blade is merely a conductor. You must have seen similar things. Carving knives, for example?"

There was a pause. Marco nodded. "Of course you are right," he said.

"Then let's get the hell out of here!"

She oriented herself as best she could and made for the nearest flight of steps.

"Where are you going?" shouted Marco.

"To find the magician!" Before you do, she added to herself. I don't want him killed. He's the only way out of here.

She trotted through empty passages, heading upward. A short flight of stairs looked familiar. She bounded up them, and there, at the end of a vaulted corridor, was the magician's chamber.

Abu Ibn Infra sat pensively cross-legged on the magic carpet, watching her carefully over the top of thin, steepled fingers. Somewhat nearer the horse-faced shape of Azrifel crouched, splay-toed.

Kin glanced around the room. There was no one else there.

Abu Ibn Infra spoke.

"Why Have Your Creatures Attacked and Slaughtered My People?" translated Azrifel.

"We had expected better treatment," said Kin.

"Why? You Come from the Place of Thieves and Liars with Two Renegade Demons—"

"They're not demons," she said sharply. "They're intelligent living creatures. They just happen to be of different races. Now, about that flying carpet—"

"They Are Demons."

Kin felt a gust of air from the far side of the room, and was in time to see two figures coalesce.

They were kung. Not perhaps perfect copies, and they moved curiously as if whatever had created them had aimed for kung shape without a knowledge of kung anatomy.

Abu had summoned demons to deal with her, and somewhere there was something that had observed that the kung shape was good for a fighter. . . .

It had added disc touches. In battle kung usually carried no more than a short sword and a small blast deflector, leaving two arms for freelance throttling. These carried a weapon in each hand, and each one was different. One even twirled a morningstar.

It would be like being hit by colliding lawnmowers.

Kin stared at the two expressionless faces, *dead* faces, and stopped herself from turning to run. She'd be running downstairs, with *those* behind her.

She raised the sword hopefully.

Something squirmed under her hand. Pain exploded up her arm and rattled her teeth. As the kung-things loped toward her the sword crackled.

Movement slowed. Through a pink glow Kin saw the demons slow as if they'd run into jelly, but there was no sound at all. Hate settled on her dreamily, comfortably, and she watched the sword come up with interest.

There was no shock when it drifted through an ax blade, and went on to shear through an arm—the flesh was gray, boneless and bloodless—and another sword.

She folded away from a snail's-pace spear, and started a long slow leap that let her slice through a neck.

She swung her feet around in time to land lightly, twist, and let the sword sweep like a scythe.

Now there was a third enemy, backing away through the red mists. The sword jerked and Kin jumped, feeling her body curve behind the blade like the tail of a comet. It struck the figure in the chest, and Kin left it there.

She drifted on and into the wall, colliding gently with a faint prickling sensation. Then she began a lazy tumble to the floor, several miles away.

It had no right to hit her so hard.

* * *

She felt as though one side of her body were one long bruise. Her shoulder muscles were screaming. Her arm suggested that it had been dragged through a sieve.

For a blissful few seconds she was able to view the clamoring sensations objectively, looking into the kaliedoscope of her own head. Then subjectivity set in with a rush.

There was a slithering noise behind her, and a soft thud. With a certain amount of agony she turned her head to see Abu sprawled against the wall, with a long red smear above him.

Kin lay cherishing the coolness of the floor. Then she used her left arm, which merely ached horribly, to walk it on its fingers to the magician's outflung hand. She uncurled his fingers from the lamp, and dragged it back until it was in front of her eyes.

It didn't look anything special. She buffed its surface with a finger.

"I Am Azrifel, Slave of the Lamp," said the demon in a singsong voice. "Your Wish Is My Command."

"Fetch me a doctor," said Kin thickly. The demon disappeared. There was a tiny thunderclap.

An agony later he reappeared. In his arms, kicking faintly and whimpering, was a small white-faced man in a black robe.

"Wass that?" said Kin.

"Johannes Angelego of the University of Toledo."

Kin picked up the lamp and hammered it on the tiles. Azrifel screamed. The small scholar echoed him, then fainted.

"I mean a physician, you horse," muttered Kin. "Take that man back and bring me a proper doctor. It's a box eight foot long, demon, with lights and dials on it. A *doctor*. Unnerstan? Hell, even a human doctor would do."

She hit the lamp again. Azrifel shrieked and disappeared.

This time he took longer. When he reappeared he carried a figure riding pickaback, and was holding a large equipment box in his arms. Kin looked up hazily at the familiar green allsuit of an intern at the Company Medical Center. The man jumped down, landing with all the athletic grace of one with unlimited access to rejuvenation treatments.

Kin recognized Jen Teremilt, his face wavering slightly as the pain closed in. Good old Jen—she'd nearly married him, a hundred and forty years ago. He'd have reached a high position in the Company's medical history if he hadn't died while hunting chaque on Sister.

His cool fingers reached out for her.

Though the carpet could easily carry the three of them—Azrifel did not appear to weigh anything—Marco insisted on ordering the flying horse to follow them closely.

"Are we ready?" said Marco.

The sun still hadn't shown above the disc, but there was enough pearly predawn light to show Kin and Silver sitting on the carpet in the middle of the cool roof.

Kin's arm felt numb. She shivered.

"Let's go," she said. She rubbed the lamp. Azrifel appeared beside her.

"Well?" he said. "What?"

"What happened to all that O Mistress stuff?" said Kin, surprised.

Marco snorted impatiently.

"All Right, Don't Get Stuffy. That Sort of Stuff Was All Right for *Him*—I Gathered You Were More Democratic." An etiquette lesson from a hundred and ninety years before jogged Kin's overloaded memory—a gentleman is someone who always says "thank you" to his robot.

"This lamp," she said. "Suppose I were to give it to you?"

The demon blinked, and thought about it. After a moment a green tongue flicked out across its dry lips.

"I Would Take It and Drop It over the Edge of the World, O Mistress," it said. "Then I Would Have Peace."

"Fly this carpet to the center of the world and I will give you the lamp," said Kin. Azrifel grinned. Kin added, "See the kung on the horse? You will note he has the magic sword. I will give him the lamp. Should you betray us in any way, no doubt he will damage the lamp in interesting ways—"

The demon shivered.

"Point Taken," he said, gloomily. "Is There No Trust in This World?"

"No," said Marco flatly.

The carpet rose and skimmed over the darkened city. Marco following closely on the flying horse.

Kin watched the houses pass below and thought:

Something looks into our minds. The magic table produced food we merely thought of. When I thought of a doctor, *it* sent Azrifel with the man I had in mind, but it wouldn't produce an autodoc. Why?

Azrifel was still crouched vacantly beside her. At the front of the carpet Silver stared blankly at nothing.

"Azrifel," said Kin, "Bring me—oh, bring me a fully equipped matrix drive MFTL ship with the latest-model dumbwaiter."

Over the com circuit she heard Marco cackle.

The demon said, "No."

"Is that a refusal? We have your lamp."

Azrifel shook his head. "It Is Not a Refusal," he said. "It Is a Statement. Oysters Cannot Fly, I Cannot Bring You Your Desire. Now Crush the Lamp If You Must."

"No anachronisms," said Marco. "Is that it?"

The demon paused before answering, as though listening to an eternal voice. Seen up close, he too was slightly blurred—like a threevee picture in the middle of a bad day for sunspots, Kin thought.

"No Nachronisms," he agreed.

"But the man called Jalo left the world and appeared two hundred light—many, many miles away," Kin corrected herself. "How?"

"I Do Not Know."

"Jalo's ship is in distant orbit," said Marco. "We could adapt the life system, cannibalize bits out of our lander, and go home in that."

"It'd take too long!"

"Perhaps not."

"What about power?"

"A thousand of these magic carpets joined edge to edge?"

"Navigation?"

"Dead reckoning. We'll be aiming at a fifty-light-year sphere from a distance of one hundred and fifty years. No trouble."

"Neat. And what about Silver?"

Marco said nothing.

When the sun came up, it was tinted with green.

They flew over a sandstorm half a mile high, which blasted through farms and towns like snow from hell.

Marco didn't say much and Silver was now saying nothing at all. She lay curled up on the carpet, looking at the sky.

They thundered over a port called Basra, where the timber of broken ships clogged the streets while the mad sea methodically destroyed the town.

Silver said: "Something shining on the horizon."

Kin wondered if she could see a faint gleam on the borders of vision. Ten minutes later she was sure.

Silver stirred again. "Leave," she ordered. "The kung must come here. With swords."

"Marco—"

"I heard. Stop the carpet. You can take the horse."

"But you know what she's asking!"

"Sure. If things get too bad, I'll have to kill her."

"How can you be so emotionless about it?"

"Why not? Better a dead sapient than a live animal. I agree with her."

"What'll happen afterward?"

He pursed his lips. "She'll reincarnate on the disc, I guess. Better a live human than a dead sha—"

"Will you stop talking like that!"

The gleam turned out to be a high dome, welded into the rock of a wide island that seemed to be mostly black sand. Kin thought she could make out the remains of a few ships half buried in the sand.

They circled it, a mile out at first, then moving closer in. Kin saw a black shape spiral down out of the sky and perch on the dome.

"That does it," she said. "Marco, I'm going in."

The kung's answer was a strangled grunt. Kin spun around in the saddle.

A few meters away Silver was rearing up on the carpet, the fur of one arm bright orange where it had caught the thrust of the sword. Her hand was around Marco's waist while he had two hands gripping her throat, and between them the sword screamed as they wrestled.

The carpet drifted on past. Kin got a brief glimpse of Silver's contorted face twisted around a saliva-barred mouth.

Kin grabbed the lamp. Azrifel appeared, standing on air, and watching the silent fighters with interest.

"Separate them," Kin ordered.

"No."

Marco somersaulted away from Silver, caught her arm in

three of his, and threw her over his shoulder. His leg bones bent like springs. Then Silver was over the edge of the carpet.

But not falling. She hung at an impossible angle in its safety field, snarling and thrashing at the air.

"No?"

"I Dare Not Go Closer to the Dome."

"I have the lamp, demon."

"I Suggest You Do Not Use It."

Kin saw Marco lift the sword and hesitate. Silver picked up leverage on sheer fresh air, and hurtled toward him.

Shand, kung and carpet disappeared.

Kin stared at the empty space. Below, the sea roared. There was nothing else around but sea, sky and dome, and the horse-faced demon hovering over nothing at all.

Finally she said: "Demon, what happens if I drop the lamp in the sea? The truth, now."

"Sometimes Fish or Crabs Will Brush Against It. Their Wishes Are Simple and Easily Fulfilled."

"What happened to the carpet?"

"It Disappeared?" said the demon uncertainly.

"I know. Why?"

"Things That Approach Too Close to the Center of the World Do So."

"You didn't tell us."

"You Didn't Ask Me."

"Where do they disappear to?"

"To? They Just *Disappear*. That Is All I Know."

"You'll know more soon," said Kin. She shoved the lamp back into her pocket and urged the horse forward—toward the dome. Azrifel whimpered.

Presently Kin disappeared.

Kin awoke at the heart of a galaxy strained through a ruby. Touch told her that she was lying on a floor like polished metal, and an old but hitherto unnamed sense assured her that she was inside something. A building. Maybe a cave.

Around her a billion pinpoints of red light glowed. They spread away from her in complicated constellations, climbed the invisible wall tens of meters away and met in the blackness overhead. Sometimes the pattern changed instantly, to be replaced by one equally red and forbidding. It was a pointillist's vision of hell.

Then Kin moved.

Stampede. The lights poured down the walls and clustered around her. She stood up and stamped a foot experimentally. Experiment was the word, and she clung to it. Be rational. Don't go mad.

She thought she had been prepared for anything. Robots, lasers, long-headed disc builders in silver suits, intelligent slimes—anything. But not these lights. It wasn't as though they lit anything but themselves.

"Get me out of here," she growled.

Flash. Now she was standing in an arched corridor, her nostrils filled with the hot metal, ozone and oil smell of machinery. The tunnel was brightly lit by a continuous strip overhead. Pipes and cables snaked along the walls, and the floor was a linear maze of rails. There were distant bangs and thumps, and everywhere there was the hum of hurtling electrons.

Kin picked a direction and walked, carefully avoiding anything that looked highly electric.

So, she told herself, this is the works. I'm down among the cogwheels of the Universe. But it's all *wrong*. The technology looks ancient. Cogwheels is about right. Good grief!

She was halfway past an alcove giving off from the main tunnel. There was movement in there. Kin started to run for cover, then thought, what the hell?

It was a robot, a big one shaped the best shape for a robot. Square. One waldo arm was groping in a square hole in the alcove's metal wall. A square panel lay on the floor.

The arm clicked back. It held something small that Kin couldn't quite see properly, which it dropped into a hopper bolted on to the robot's side. A drawer slid out just above the hopper, and this time Kin got a good view of the objects nestling in its padded interior. The arm waved uncertainly above them, then selected one gingerly and carried it into the hole.

While the machine was engaged in its mysterious activities Kin strolled forward and picked one of the objects out of the rack in the drawer. It was about the size of an egg. One end was studded with hundreds of pins, and inside was a filigree of wires, tubes and grids.

Kin had seen things like it in a museum. It was a valve, a sort of neolithic integrated circuit. Only this was a valve such as might be built by someone who had never developed the transistor, so that more and ingenuity had been devoted to perfecting the existing technology.

It made Kin think of Ehftnic computers. The ehfts had never discovered electronics *but* they needed computers for their complex religio-banking organizations. So an Ehftnic computer was a thousand highly trained ehfts, each one handling a small part of the math. It worked.

But she'd be dipped in dogshit before she'd believe that the disc was built by a thermionic-valve technology.

The robot's arm whirred out of the wall. The panel was picked up and slotted into place with surprising speed. Almost before Kin could react her new friend was rumbling off down the tunnel. It moved at a fast walking pace. She followed.

She would survive. If They were going to kill her, They would have done it already. She'd live. Provided she didn't bank on it, she'd live.

Once they passed another cuboid robot, wielding some kind of tool over some kind of exposed circuitry. It could have been a soldering iron. It could have been a printed circuit. Kin couldn't stop to check.

Then Kin's robot reached a robot-shaped slot in the wall. Kin had a brief glimpse of sockets at the back of the slot before the robot reversed in, with all the painstaking care of a fornicating porcupine. It stopped humming. Patently, the repairman had gone dormant.

Kin considered for some time. The tunnels seemed endless. She could wander around in them for days. Then she'd die. But there was an alternative. . . . She went back down the tunnel until she found the soldering robot. Wrenching off one of its arms was difficult, but she managed. She used it to hit the thing until it stopped humming. As an encore she tossed the arm at the exposed circuitry, which sparked satisfyingly.

Then she waited.

When a small, hemispherical robot-repair robot rolled up a few minutes later she overturned it. It hummed at her reproachfully.

The next one was a pear-shaped, multilensed blob traveling along a rail, near the ceiling of the tunnel. Kin tried to bring it down with pieces of robot, but it swung away hastily.

At least she had made her presence felt. *Someone* must repair the robots that repaired the robot-repairing robots. All it took was time.

Hours passed before a tanklike machine arrived. It was dented and lacked paneling, and bore the stumps of various delicate manipulatory appendages. If this was the ultimate repairer, Kin supposed, then sheer time could have caused its battered state.

On the other hand, the fact that Marco was sitting on its hull with a robotic arm trailing wires in each hand could have had something to do with it.

"Perhaps there just aren't any facilities for dealing with humans who get into the machinery," said Kin.

Marco grunted, but didn't look up from his work. He was doing something neolithic with a length of robot innards, using the small repair hemisphere as a hammer.

"There must be," he said. "This world must be studded with hidden air ducts, ventilators, power shafts. Humans poke into everywhere. Anyway, we were brought here, remember? Subsequently to ignore us is impolite."

He stood up. "Coming?"

"Where?"

"Anywhere with delicate circuitry. This"—he waved a robot limb—"is insulated. For short-circuiting."

"And the other thing?" asked Kin, her heart sinking.

It was a connected series of arm sections, terminating in a crude but lethal blade. Marco hefted it experimentally.

"Huh? It's a weapon, obviously."

"You were maybe expecting to meet some antipersonnel robots?" Kin said icily.

Marco had the decency not to meet her gaze.

"I was thinking of Silver," he said wretchedly. "Well? Do you imagine she's found anything to eat yet? And have you got any better ideas?"

He set off along a tributary tunnel, and called back, "Anyway, it can't have escaped your notice that these tunnels are lit. Robots don't need light."

Kin shrugged. Perhaps soldering robots needed light. A little light destruction to attract attention was one thing, however—intelligent action in the circumstances. But Marco looked ready to smash the whole disc.

In the distance she saw him hacking at cables. This

wasn't action to attract attention—this was Marco vs. the Universe.

What was happening up on the surface? A plague of flies? A rain of frogs? All the seas running dry? The extinction of the dodo?

Now she was running. Marco was a terrible figure wreathed in smoke, hacking at a solid cliff of planet-sized circuit. There was a jerkiness about his movements that told Kin all she needed to know. Marco had gone mad. Or at least gone kung.

She stopped when his blade swept a few inches from her throat.

"They want to play games, eh?" he croaked. "Put us on the spot, watch our reactions, eh? *I'll* show them."

One free hand swept his club into a circuit board, which exploded.

"I'll show *them*."

Kin swayed back, her eyes on the tip of the blade. Then a movement to the right of Marco's private smoke cloud made her look away. Marco saw her expression, and hesitated for a fraction of a second too long.

Silver leaped. Marco disappeared as the huge paddlelike arms swept around in a bone-grinding hug, then appeared again with three arms flailing at the shand's head. Silver screamed, and one foot came up with claws out to disembowel the enemy. Marco's bowels had already gone with the rest of him for Silver's eyes. While the shand staggered across the floor clawing at the demon atop her, Kin saw Marco's fourth arm swing up with his pike.

It twirled gracefully, the blade drifting through the hot air like the scythe of death. Then it buried itself in a power cable.

There was a sound like the snapping of locusts. Silver and Marco appeared for a moment like a tableau, Silver a big fluffy ball as every hair stood out from her body.

Kin scrabbled on the floor for Marco's anti-disc weapon with its insulated handle. It took all her strength to knock the vibrating pike out of his hand. When it came away, the two aliens collapsed.

Aliens, she thought. I called them aliens. Oh, shit. She knelt down and sought for signs of life. Something vague was happening in Silver's chest, but she didn't know where even to begin looking for either of Marco's hearts.

The lights overhead dwindled to a sickly orange glow. There were footsteps behind Kin—strange, rattling steps. She turned, still crouching, to see the tall figure that had appeared behind her.

The most obvious thing was the weapon that was sweeping down toward her. Instinctively she flung up an arm, which was still holding Marco's club. The scythe hit it hard, and shivered into pieces.

Kin started to laugh. The thing in front of her was a skeleton in a black bathrobe, grinning perplexedly at a wooden handle that now had no blade. Who were They trying to scare?

The scythe handle in Death's white claws *flowed*. What it became was at least appropriate to the age of genocide, and Kin had time to wonder where They had found the pattern. There were two rows of oscillating teeth and a brisk little engine.

A power scythe. Kin had used them herself to clear scrub on new worlds.

Death advanced. Had he lunged Kin wouldn't have survived, but ancient habits die hard. He swung, instead. And Kin dived forward. She heard the power scythe crash down behind her and gyrate across the floor as she stared up into eyeless sockets. Struggling, she brought one knee up—a pointless tactic that merely jarred her kneecap. Death had no balls.

A necklace of bony fingers closed around her throat. She lashed out with the back of her hand, willing the blow home. It hit Death in the face, and then there was something like an explosion in a domino factory.

Kin was standing alone. There was a black robe on the floor in front of her, and a few pieces of bone scattered around. They disappeared in a series of small thunderclaps. A larger one marked the disappearance of Marco and Silver.

Kin disappeared, too.

A minute later a couple of cuboid robots trundled along the tunnel and started to clean up the mess.

Now she was in a—

"No," she said. "No more. I give in. Do you know how long it was since I last had a drink?"

A glass of water appeared hovering in the air in front o

her. Kin wasn't particularly surprised. She caught it gingerly, and drank it. When she tried to hang the glass in the air it plummeted down and smashed.

Now she was in a—call it a control room. The disc control room. This had to be it.

It was surprisingly small. It could have been the flight deck of a medium-large ship, except that a ship would have more screens and switches. This had one screen and one bank of switches, in front of a deep black chair. Over the chair was what could have been a computer-link helmet.

"Oh no," she said. "Not me. I'm not putting that on."

The screen flickered and a word appeared.

BETS?

Kin moved forward and got a better view of the chair. It was a disturbing complicated shape, and looked almost alive.

Its occupant was dead. Not offensively dead, because the air in the room was crisp and dry and had expertly mummified him, but undeniably dead. If he had believed in reincarnation, he'd come back as a corpse.

There was an old wound on one withered arm. It didn't look fatal, but there were antique bloodstains on the floor. He could have bled to death, but that seemed a derisive death for a disc master.

If he *was* a disc master. Somehow Kin had never brought herself to think of the disc's overlords as humans, but the man in the chair was human enough. Given a heavy shave and a fresh skin he could have called anyone cousin.

The screen in front of the chair blurred, then produced a word. It hung in front of Kin, glowing pitifully.

HELP

Marco crouched in the semidarkness when he next heard the voice.

After a while he surfaced from the mists of rage enough to realize that it was talking to him. It was familiar. The ape-descended woman?

"Kin Arad?" he croaked.

"Marco, where's Silver?" the voice insisted.

Marco's eyes felt like fire pits, but the light from the millions of red glows around him suited his vision. He saw a shape a few meters away, eclipsing a constellation on the floor.

"The bear thing is here. She is breathing."

"Marco," said the air. "I don't know how good I am at this thing. You'll have to help. Don't move."

The air stirred in front of the kung, and there was a knife. Three of Marco's hands caught it before it hit the ground. In the red light, he stared dully at the jewel-encrusted handle.

"Don't waste time," said the ape voice. "I want you to cut a piece out of Silver. Don't be too enthusiastic. Hide will do, but the flesh would be better."

Memories were dripping into Marco's mind. He looked at the knife, then thought about Silver.

"Not on your life," he said flatly.

"Do it. The next knife will arrive at speed if you don't, and you'd better believe me."

With a roar of rage and frustration Marco bounded forward and slashed at Silver's arm. The big body may have quivered slightly.

"That'll do. The blood on the knife will do. Let go of the knife, Marco. Let go of the knife. Let-go-of-the-knife."

Marco was thirsty. He hadn't eaten in memory. His skin itched in the warm dry air. He was damned if he'd let go of a weapon. If he thought about it at all, that was what he thought.

"Okay. We'll do it the hard way."

There was just something about the voice that made Marco loose his grip on the handle. Thus it was that when the knife popped out of existence, it merely stripped the flesh of his palm instead of taking his hand off at the wrist.

Methodically he gripped his wrist to stop the blood flow, and let the pain batter outside his brain. He was still staring at the wound when a rush of air and a thump made him look up.

Something long and bloody was lying on the floor beside Silver. And the shand's arm was moving slowly. It fumbled around the meat, gripped it, pulled it dreamily to a mouth strung with saliva.

Silver ate.

"Where are we?" said Marco at last.

Kin's voice said, "I'm not entirely sure. Are you okay?"

"I should like a drink. And some food. You had me slice the shand to get a protein sample?"

"Yes. Don't move."

Something like a squashy bulb of water appeared beside Marco, and bounced limply on the floor. He picked it up and bit into it with shameful haste.

"Food now," said Kin. Another bulb, filled with red sludge, rolled obscenely across the floor. Marco tried it. It tasted like solid boredom.

"It's the best I can manage," said Kin. "About the only damage you did was upset the disc master's dumbwaiter circuits. I've got robots repairing them, but until then the menu can just about manage to be unexciting."

"Silver has fared better," said Marco indistinctly.

"I told you I hadn't got time for niceties," said Kin. "She's eating shand, cultured from her own cells. Don't ask me how it was done in seconds, I only gave the order. It might be an idea not to tell her, though."

"Yes. You are in a position of influence?"

"You could say that."

"Good. *Get me out of here!*"

There was a pause. Then he heard Kin say. "I've been giving a lot of thought to that."

"You've been giving a lot of thought to it?"

"Yes. I've been giving a lot of thought to it. You're in a sort of hold-for-study chamber. There's no way in or out except by teleportation, and if you knew what I know about that you'd rather stay in there and starve. I daren't cut in in case you're harmed. So, all things considered . . ."

A long shape exploded into being a meter from Marco, and landed heavily. He picked it up and looked at it suspiciously.

"It looks like an industrial molecule stripper," he said.

"It is. I suggest you use it with caution."

Marco grimaced in the hellish light and pointed the thing. A section of chamber wall became a fine fog. He switched off hastily, and looked around for Silver.

The shand was kneeling, holding her head.

"How do you feel?" said Marco, in a concerned tone. He held the stripper lightly, not quite pointing it at Silver. The shand squinted at him vaguely.

"Odd things been happening. . . ." she began.

Marco helped her to her feet, a more or less token gesture since she weighed ten times his weight—and he needed one hand to keep the stripper not quite pointing at her.

"Right now, can you walk?"

She could stagger. Marco peered out of the chamber, into a dimly lit tunnel. Two small cuboid robots were fretting over the still-settling dust of the wall. He glanced back at Silver, and opted to point the stripper's flared nozzle at a questing waldo.

"Lay off the hardware," said the robot, backing away.

"Kin Arad?" said Marco.

"Marco, that weapon is for your own peace of mind. But if you use it, I'll rip your arms off from here. And I can."

Marco considered this for several moments, while Silver climbed laboriously out of the chamber. Then he shrugged with all four shoulders, and let the weapon thump on the floor.

"Monkey logic," he said. "I'll never understand it."

"I thought you thought you were human," said the robot with Kin's voice.

"So? All the thinking in the worlds doesn't change some things."

"*Cogito ergo kung,*" said the robot. "Follow me, please."

They fell in behind it as it rolled off along the tunnel.

An hour later they were still walking. They had crossed wide metal chasms on lattice bridges and crouched in alcoves as giant machines thundered down side tunnels. On one occasion the little cube had beckoned them to follow it onto a lift platform. At the next level down the lift had stopped again and a dozen humming golden cylinders had drifted on, smelling of ozone.

They followed narrow walkways between topless towering machines, which boomed.

"Krells," said Silver.

"Huh?"

The shand grinned. "Didn't you ever see *Forbidden Planet*? Human movie. They remade it five, six times. I had a walk-on part in one, before I went to college."

"Can't say I recall anything."

". . . I had to thump doors, mostly, and roar . . . had to share my dressing room with the robot, too. He was human."

"A human robot?"

"The rest of the cast were actor robots, you see. But there was this robot in the plot, and they couldn't find a robot who could act . . . robotlike. They had to hire a human. There was a very impressive scene inside a big machine built by the Krells, I think it was. Just like this. Krells, you understand, being fictional creatures invented for the purpose of the movie. . . ." Silver broke off when she saw Marco's face.

He sighed. "We have been around humans too long, you and I," he said. "We have been tainted by their madnesses."

"I thought you were brought up on Earth. Are you not legally human?"

"My race papers are up there in the rest of the ship. Big deal."

Silver grunted. "Consider yourself a cosmopolitan, then."

"What does that really mean, my friend?"

"It means the voluntary subjugation of one's radical awareness in the light of the basic unity of sapient kind."

Marco growled. "It doesn't mean that at all. It means that *we* learn to speak languages that monkey tongues can handle, and *we* get along in their world. Ever see a human act like a shand, or a kung?"

"No," Silver conceded. "But on the other hand, Kin Arad is free and we were imprisoned. Humans always take the lead. Humans always get what they want. I like humans. My race likes humans. Maybe if we didn't like humans, we'd be dead. What's that?"

Marco followed her gaze. Half a mile away a tower loomed above the city-sized machines. It seemed to be made of giant balls stuck one atop another, and it glowed dull red. Silver pointed out the robots that clustered on the gantries that surrounded it, but Marco had to be content with a vague, eye-watering impression of something huge and ominous.

"A giant coffee percolator?" he hazarded.

Silver shouted at the little robot, which had rolled on ahead. It reversed neatly.

Silver indicated the stack of spheres that disappeared into the roof of the cavern.

"Basically," it said in Kin's voice, "it's a simple device for heating rock to melting point and ejecting it under pressure."

"Why?" said Marco.

"Volcano," said the robot.

"All that," said the kung, "to give the disc volcanoes? Madness!"

The robot rolled away.

"You say that now," it said. "You wait until you see the earthquake machines."

The journey under the disc took two days, as far as Marco and Silver could calculate. Sometimes they rode, crouching on flat trucks that glided along low tunnels with agonizing slowness, but more often they walked. Climbed. Inched along ledges. Ran like hell across switchyards, where subdisc machines shunted and thundered on errands of their own.

Sometimes they came across dumbwaiters, perched incongruously in the whirring underworld. They had a new look, unlike their surroundings, which were worn. Well looked after, carefully maintained, but worn.

Marco raised the subject while they were sitting with their backs against a dumbwaiter.

"I know," he said. "If the disc people had an industrial revolution and then took a look at the underside of their world, it'd scare the life out of them."

Silver chewed on another mouthful of what, Marco presumed, was lightly cooked shand.

"It seemed remarkably remiss of the disc builders to allow this dereliction," she said. "I have noticed quite a number of obviously broken-down devices. Surely they could be repaired?"

"Who repairs the machines that do the repairing?" said Marco. "A machine like the disc must blow a whole lot of fuses in a hundred years or so. What do you do when the robot that repairs the machines that makes the parts for the factory that builds the robots that services the waldoes that makes the fuses crashes its cog? Unless you get periodic servicing from outside, the disc gradually breaks down."

"We could ask the robot," said Silver.

It was a sick joke. The robot would answer any direct question about the mechanical scenery—they had been treated to a ten-minute lecture on the tide-regulation machinery, for example—but ignored all the others. Marco had toyed with the idea of prising its lid off with something, but allowed caution to get the better of him.

"The place with the red lights must have been out near the disc rim," said Silver. "I have a feeling we're approaching the hub again. Perhaps we can ask Kin."

The robot, which had been sitting silently a few meters away, rolled forward.

"We are refreshed?" it asked cheerfully. "We will proceed?"

They stood up stiffly. The cuboid robot led them along a catwalk that opened onto a wide circular gallery, brilliantly lit. Most of the light came from the luminous mist overhead, but an appreciable amount came from the tiny actinic sun.

It floated perhaps a hundred meters over a perfect relief model of the disc surface, several hundred meters across. Except that relief maps didn't have tiny clouds, trailing minute shadows across the land. Marco had never seen them with active volcanoes, either.

There was no railing to the gallery. The disc map glittered a meter below it, sunlight glinting off seas that looked disconcertingly real.

Marco stared down for a long time. Then he said, "I give up. It's beautiful. What's it for?"

"One thinks of architect's models," rumbled Silver. "However, let me draw your attention to a flaw. See over there, just beyond the inland sea?"

Marco squinted, and gave up. "No," he said. "The disc builders either had damn good eyesight or all this was just for show."

He looked around for the robot. It wasn't there.

"We wish to view the disc map more closely," Silver was saying to the empty air. Something like a flying slab of glass glided around the map from the far side and hovered in front of her. She stepped aboard gingerly. Under her weight it didn't even wobble.

"I see it," said Marco, "but I don't believe it. How did you do it?"

"Just a knack," said Silver. "I think I'm getting to understand the way things work around here. Coming?"

The glass carpet responded neatly to Silver's spoken directions. It skimmed across the map mere centimeters from the clouds. Marco had a strange urge to reach down and stir some into a cyclone. The map was frighteningly real. If he leaned over and touched it, would a giant hand appear in the disc sky?

When the shand spoke again he looked down obediently through the glass.

There was scarred land down there, burned and broken. And in the center of it was a neat round hole.

Later Silver found that raising the platform slightly magnified the scene immediately beneath. There appeared to be no limit to the resolving power. There were people down there, microscopic figures that were almost immobile.

Only *almost*. Every second the scene flickered, and the figures took up slightly different positions. Marco spent an age entranced at the sight of a homunculus cutting wood. *Flick*—the ax in the air—flick—biting into the tree—flick—back in the air; and a wedge of raw wood bitten by magic out of the trunk.

"It could be done," he said, half to himself. "All you'd have to do is correlate sensory inputs and keep reprojecting them as a hologram."

"You'd need many inputs."

"Billions. You'd have to plug into the cognitive center of every living creature."

"Have you noticed the blank patches?"

"Maybe a bird wasn't looking in that direction at the time."

Silver nodded gravely, and looked around the big map hall.

"Presumably the map of the disc also includes its own miniature disc map," she said slowly. She met Marco's gaze with a quiet smile. Then she ordered the platform to go to the map's hub. Neither doubted that the map hall was at the hub.

They looked down at the dome. Silver tried some commands, which appeared to have no effect. So she lowered the platform.

Staring down between their feet they saw earth and metal melt and drift aside. Disc machinery rose and faded away. There was something now, the edge of something. . . .

There was a little round disc. At its center was a gray-and-white speck, which resolved into two figures. One was big and furry, the other wiry and thin as a twig. Both were staring intently at something between their feet. . . .

Flick. The wiry one was looking up now, at the miniature gallery that encircled the map of the map. *Flick*. There was a figure there. *Flick*. It raised a hand. *Flick*.

* * *

"Hi," said Kin.

Silver was not expert in human expressions, but by the look of her the woman had not been sleeping. In fact she was swaying slightly.

"Glad you could make it," she said. "I couldn't get the computers to teleport you; there's a thirty percent chance the power would fail while you were out of phase. Follow me. There isn't a lot of time left."

"We—" began Marco.

Kin shook her head violently. "No we didn't," she said. "Come on!"

The kung started to protest again, and Silver gripped him firmly by a couple of arms. Kin was already hurrying down a tunnel leading off the hall.

It emerged in a metal cave half as big again as the one they had just left. It contained a spacecraft. At least, that was the first impression. . . .

It didn't have any motors. Apart from strangely large altitude jets in about the right places for altitude jets, the hull seemed to be all cabin, with enough windows to grow grapes. Cuboid robots were still clustered around it. One of them was spraying paint on the landing gear. Two others were busy on a stubby wing.

Kin was already aboard. Snarling, Marco bounded up the short ladder and saw her sitting at the horseshoe-shaped instrument consol. Wires trailed away from it to boxes bolted haphazardly around the interior of the cabin. In the center of the floor a regiment of tiny cubes were engaged in feverish activity around a tangle of wires and metal shapes. One of them butted Marco politely on the foot until he moved.

"Silver, shut that door," said Kin. "Hurry! And now pray to any convenient gods."

She turned and addressed the air, in a tone of voice that made it clear it was not the others she was talking to.

"We're ready."

The reply came from everywhere.

WE HAVE A BARGAIN?

"It's a bargain," said Kin. There was a pause. The ship trembled slightly. Marco looked out and saw the cave walls slipping past.

"Don't say anything rash," said Kin. "Don't even *think*, if you want to get home. Have a little faith, will you? Please?"

Sudden sunlight filled the cabin. Looking up, Marco and Silver saw a square of golden sky appear as sections of the roof slid back. The ship accelerated upward on its section of floor.

By their feet a small robot tugged a length of tubing out of the heap in the center of the cabin. One of its many arms swung down, hesitated, gripped the tube. The metal broke where it touched.

Silver jerked her head forward sharply as something tickled her ears. When she looked round cautiously she was eyeball to scanner with a little metal cube which was hanging from the cabin roof by three arms. It had no face, but managed to look embarrassed. Its fourth arm held a pair of calipers.

Marco hissed and struck out at another machine that was trying to climb up his leg. It landed on its back, scrabbling at the deck with all six arms.

Kin laughed hysterically.

"Don't be childish." she gasped. "When we flip into interspace you'd like to be in a contour couch, wouldn't you? All they want are your measurements. *Do it!*"

Marco opened his mouth to protest, and something touched his face. Looking down, he saw a metal tape unrolling on its way to the deck. He looked up. A robot was dangling above his head. He sighed.

The ship rose into daylight. It emerged in the middle of a black sand beach, with the copper dome of the hub behind it. The sea moved lazily a few meters away. There was a shudder as the lift platform locked.

Now the cubes were spraying foam over three structures of curved tubing which they had bolted to the floor. The foam congealed into about the right-sized hollows for a shand, a kung and a human.

"We've got a little time until lift-off," said Kin, and stood up. "Has anybody got any questions? Yeah. I thought you might. Okay, but get in the couches."

"You don't expect me to get us into interspace from the disc surface?" asked Marco. "We wouldn't have a chance!"

"You did it from Kung," said Kin, settling into her couch.

"Kung hasn't got a damn great dome over the sky!"

"No. I don't expect to flip yet, anyway. We need the couches for the primary launch."

"But who is going to be at the controls? I can't reach them from here!"

"No one is going to be at the controls. There aren't any for the launch. Trust me."

"No controls and you want me to trust you?"

"Yes. I want you to trust me."

Marco lay down and reached for the couch straps. Silver was already prone. They lay in silence for a while.

Then Kin said, "Marco, can you see that round screen from your couch?"

"I see it."

"It's radar. Keep an eye on it. And now, perhaps I owe you an explanation. . . ."

HELP, said the screen.

Trying not to think about it, Kin lifted the occupant out of the chair and sat down in front of the pleading letters. Keeping the hovering helmet in the top of her eye, she ran her hand over the arm.

Nothing happened, except that the screen now read YOU ARE KIN ARAD.

"That's—" Kin's voice sounded faint in the closeness of the room. She cleared her throat. "That is correct," she said. "Who are you?"

WE BELIEVE YOU HAVE REFERRED TO US AS THE DISC MASTERS, ALTHOUGH WE CALL OURSELVES THE COMMITTEE.

"It's got a nice democratic ring about it. Let me see you."

IS THAT AN EXPRESS WISH?

"Well, I've come a long way to meet you. This is hardly an intimate conversation, you must admit." Kin looked around; looking for doors, hidden cameras. The walls were blank.

YOU MISUNDERSTAND US. WE ARE MACHINES. COMPUTERS, JAGO JALO CALLED US. WE FAIL TO UNDERSTAND YOUR SURPRISE.

"I'm not surprised," lied Kin.

THEN WE SUGGEST YOU SUE YOUR FACE FOR SLANDER.

"Why do you need help? It's me that needs help. What has happened to my friends?"

THEY ARE SAFELY IN PROTECTIVE CUSTODY. THEY WERE TOO VIOLENT TO BE ALLOWED TO ROAM LOOSE, OF COURSE. DO YOU WISH THEM TO BE FREED, AND FOR US TO PROVIDE YOU WITH TRANSPORT TO YOUR HOME WORLD? IF YOU SO ORDER, IT WILL BE DONE.

"I can order you?"

YOU SIT IN THE CHAIR. THERE IS NO OTHER INCUMBENT. YOU ARE THE CHAIRMAN. THEREFORE YOU CAN GIVE THE ORDERS. WE IMPLORE YOU TO DO SO.

"You can build me a ship?"

WE BUILT A SHIP FOR JAGO JALO. WE ASSISTED HIM, DESPITE ALL THAT HE DID. CHOICE DOES NOT EXIST FOR MACHINES IN MATTERS OF THIS NATURE. JALO CHOSE TO FLEE THE DISC RATHER THAN LEARN MORE ABOUT IT.

Kin considered this carefully. When she spoke, she spoke slowly.

"You will give me a ship, but if I choose to leave the disc you won't tell me any more about it?"

YES.

"But you said I could give the orders."

YES. HOWEVER, WE BELIEVE WE WILL SHORTLY EXPERIENCE A SLIGHT MALFUNCTION IN OUR AUDTORY CIRCUITORY. IT MAY PREVENT US FROM HEARING ANY SUBSEQUENT ORDERS.

Kin smiled. "Then there's no choice, is there? Not against blackmail. Tell me about the disc."

"Kin," said Marco urgently. "There's something on the screen."

"It's about time," replied Kin. "Don't worry."

"Yeah, I remember. Trust you. It's bloody big. What is it?'

"It's our launch vehicle."

Kin leaned back in the oh-so-easy chair and stared at the blank screen for a long time.

"You're wearing out," she said. "That's why the seas are going mad and the climate's shifting. I understand that. The disc is a machine. Machines have a finite life. That's why the Company builds planets."

PLANETS HAVE A FINITE LIFE.

"A longer one. They don't start to squeak on their bearings after half a million years."

YOU GLOAT?

"No. I keep thinking of a few hundred million people on a spaceship the size of a world, and then I think of all the things that can go wrong with a ship. I don't gloat, I tremble with fear. And rage."

She stood up and stomped across the room to ease the cramp in her muscles. It had been a long session, a subterranean travelogue of disc machinery. The earthquake machines stuck in her memory. All that ingenuity, to reproduce what any half-sized world did naturally. And the demons . . . well, at least she'd put a stop to the demons.

There was a click as Marco undid his straps and leaped toward the horseshoe panel. He peered at the screen, then glared out of the cabin.

"Where the hell is it? It's gone off the screen. What was it, Kin? The blip was bigger than a—"

Whump. Beyond the windows the seashore exploded into a sandstorm.

Marco craned his head and looked up. Darkness filled the cabin as the sun was eclipsed.

Whump.

Marco looked up at talons dropping out of the sky when the impossible bird stooped. Talons big enough to grip a ship. He made a small noise in his throat and took a dive in the direction of his couch.

Whump. Scrabble. Whump. Whumpwhump. Whumpwhump.

The ship creaked as the claws took it gently. Then it bounded upward in a series of boneshaking jerks.

The dome of the hub swung crazily below and whirled away. The disc dropped after it, teetering across the sky until it was a blue-and-ocher wall. It paused there, then plunged back under the ship to loom for a moment on the other side. *Whump.*

Kin concentrated on the view above, to take her mind off the lurching, jerking universe. The talons all but covered the roof port, but she got occasional glimpses of the huge white wings, beating now with the slow rhythm of a tide.

Sound filled the cabin. It began in the painful ultrasonic, swooping down the scale like wet fingers being dragged across the windows of the soul.

High above the disc the roc stood on the air and sang.

There would be no more demons. She could see why there had been demons—demons were an idea that worked—but there would be no more.

The ones Kin had met had been almost human compared

with some of the things force-bred in the quiet green laboratories under the hub. They policed the disc, haunted the hidden air vents and access shafts to the machinery, chased the venturesome from the rim. Occasionally they kidnapped a new Chairman, for the Committee.

The Chairmen. Kin stared at the blank screen, then glanced up at the hovering direct-link helmet over the chair. She had no intention of trying it for size, and the computers hadn't pressed her, but they had shown her how it was used.

The computers ran the disc. They adjusted its tides, circulated its waters, counted its falling sparrows, toiled and spun for the lilies of the fields. But the disc's builders had constructed them as servile mechanisms, lest the disc become too mechanical. A human had to tell them what to do.

In the seventy thousand years of the disc's history there had been two hundred and eighty Chairmen, thrust in terror under the helmet. It gave them cold new knowledge.

Kin said she didn't believe it.

"You couldn't take a neolithic farmer and turn him into a planetary engineer," she protested.

WE COULD. THE DISC BUILDERS CONSTRUCTED US CLEVERLY.

"You won't even tell me about the builders!"

The screen went blank.

Whump. Kin gripped the edges of the couch. *Whump.* The roc didn't fly, it simply bullied its way through the upper air, shoveling it aside with a sneer.

Talking was difficult when g-forces slapped and banged with a horrible rhythm. Silver managed it with the least discomfort.

"I don't believe it either," she said. "I can see what a device like the disc would need." *Whump.* "Need a sapient caretaker. No machines could handle all the problems that might crop." *Whump.* "Might crop up. But unless the creature was already a technical sophisticate, he would simply become mad."

Kin braced herself for the next wingbeat. It didn't come. Beyond the window she could see the roc's wing outstretched, the tips of the huge feathers vibrating in the slipstream. The bird was starting its glide.

Half the disc was spread before the canted cabin. Kin rolled out of her couch and swayed across the trembling deck until she could grasp a bulkhead.

The world was a bowl of jewels flung across the sky. Ahead, wearing the setting sun like the gemstone on a ring, was the Rim Ocean.

Roc slid on down the sky, staring at the sun with terrible bird eyes. Sometimes she shrugged her shoulders to dislodge the ice, which flashed and tumbled as it began the long fall.

Kin knelt on the floating platform and watched the microfigures of Silver and Marco thread their way through the tunnels.

Elsewhere disc machines were lurching into action. She wondered what would have happened if some medieval farmer was Chairman now. Could he have helped the computers start the long repair?

She stood up and ordered the platform to the walkway at the rim of the map hall, and hurried up the worn stairs to the interface room.

HELLO, said the screen.

"You don't need me," said Kin. "I've given you all the instructions you need to repair yourself. It will take you a long time, but you can do it without affecting the biosp—oh boy, the biohemisphere, I suppose—too much. But you can't go on like it—not unless you get fresh materials from outside."

WE KNOW. ENTROPY IS AGAINST US.

"You can't go on cannibalizing old machines for spare parts. You may last another hundred years, that's all."

WE KNOW.

"Do you care about the people on the surface?"

THEY ARE OUR CHILDREN.

Kin stared at the glowing letters. Then she said softly: "Tell me about Jago Jalo. He must have seemed a godsend."

YES. WE WERE ALREADY AWARE THAT THE DISC WAS DOOMED. IN THOSE DAYS WE MAINTAINED AN ARRESTOR SCREEN AGAINST METEORITES. IT WAS COMPARATIVELY EASY TO EXTRACT THE RESIDUAL VELOCITY FROM HIS SHIP. WE WATCHED HIM BRING HIS SMALLER SHIP WITHIN THE VAULT OF HEAVEN. UNFORTUNATELY WE COULD NOT CONTACT HIM. THAT SHOULD HAVE MADE US SUSPICIOUS.

"You allowed him to land, though."

UNFORTUNATELY HIS SHIP ATTRACTED THE ATTENTION OF A ROC DURING THE DESCENT.

"A roc?"

A LARGE BIRD.

"I don't believe it," said Marco. "I see it, but I don't believe it. It's going to take us home, is that it?"

Below them land flashed past in a dusty blur. There was a brief impression of surf and then the roc was arrowing out to sea.

"Didn't you see the big egg in that garden where you were caged?" said Kin weakly. "Didn't you wonder what laid it? Of course it can't take us home, it's just a big bird. I saw the specifications, back in the hub."

"It seems a little stupid to say this in the circumstances," said Silver, "but such a creature could not exist in flesh and blood. It would collapse under its own weight."

"It doesn't weigh more than five tonnes," said Kin. "It's one of the disc builders' finest constructions. It's alive. It's got sinews like Line cord and its bones are pneumatic. Just tubes filled with gas under pressure. The computers showed me. Marvelous, isn't it?"

"Why is it losing height? We'll land in the sea," said Marco.

"Yes," said Kin. "I should get back into your couch if I were you."

"You mean we *are* going to land in the sea?"

Marco looked down at the rushing waves. They were low enough for every crest to be visible. Then he looked at what, on the disc, had to be called the horizon. The sun was just a red glow, half hidden by strips of cloud, tipping the wavetops with fire. Marco thought.

"Oh no," he said. "Tell me I'm wrong. Tell me you're not planning to do what I think you are planning to do. . . ."

"If it helps you any," said Kin, "Jago Jalo was insane even by the standards of an insane age."

IT BECAME OBVIOUS. WE HAD NOT CONSIDERED THAT ANY RACE WOULD SEND ITS MADMEN INTO SPACE.

"In a ship like his, only a madman would go."

HE CAME TO THE HUB WITH A DEMOUNTED GEOLOGICAL LASER. HE KILLED THE CHAIRMAN OF THE TIME.

"You didn't try to stop him?"

WE WERE NOT INSTRUCTED TO DO SO. BESIDES, THE MAN WAS OBVIOUSLY FROM A TECHNOLOGICAL CULTURE. WE HAD TO WEIGH THE FUTURE OF THE DISC. HE ORDERED US TO BUILD HIM A SHIP. IT WAS NOT DIFFICULT. WE CALCULATED THAT IF WE ASSISTED JAGO JALO BACK TO HIS HOME WORLD IT WOULD NOT BE LONG BEFORE WE HAD FURTHER VISITORS. THEREFORE WE SENT WITH HIM ONE OF OUR SPY BIRDS—THE RAVENS, THE EYES OF GOD, OUR BEAUTIFULLY CREATED BIRDS.

"Then why didn't you contact us as soon as we arrived? Hell, I've had fleas, I've nearly been burned alive, I was shoved in a seraglio—"

WE DECIDED TO OBSERVE YOU FIRST. WE COULD NOT BE SURE THAT JALO WAS AN EXCEPTION. AND THEN THE FOUR-ARMED CREATURE ADDED WEIGHT TO OUR SUSPICIONS.

Kin watched the letters fade. She said: "You know that we can build worlds. Proper worlds. Planets. We could build a planet for the disc people. You know it is a fair copy of my home world?"

YES.

"Do you know why?"

YES.

"Will you tell me?"

The screen stayed blank for several seconds. Then it was filled with words, so many that the computers had had to reduce the size of the letters. Kin stood up and read:

YOU WISH TO KNOW ABOUT THE DISC BUILDERS. YOU WISH TO KNOW THE REASONS BEHIND THE CONSTRUCTION OF THE DISC. WE CAN TELL YOU. BUT IT IS OUR ONLY BARGAINING COUNTER ON BEHALF OF OUR CHILDREN. IT IS POSSIBLE THAT YOU COULD LEAVE AND RETURN TO PLUNDER THE DISC, AS JALO HAD INTENDED. WE COULD NOT STOP YOU. YET WE REALIZE THAT KNOWLEDGE IS A PRIZE YOU GREATLY DESIRE. WE WILL GIVE YOU KNOWLEDGE. YOU WILL BUILD A NEW WORLD FOR OUR PEOPLE.

Kin had already been considering it. It would mean building a G-type star within a few light-minutes of the disc, unless there was a suitable one that could be moved. . . .

"We'd need access to disc technology," she said. "Teleportation, the force-grow vat theories, the lot."

YOU WOULD HAVE IT, OF COURSE.

"Then you will have your new world. If the Company won't do it, I could float a Company of my own with that bait. I could go to one of the small operators—yes, I'll do it."

WE HAVE A BARGAIN.

"Just like that? You don't need any—well, I guess I can't give you any sureties," said Kin, surprised.

WE HAVE OBSERVED YOU. WE ESTIMATE THERE IS A 99.87 PER CENT CHANCE THAT YOU WILL HONOR THE BARGAIN. DON THE HELMET.

Kin looked up at the padded metal rim above her head.

WE TRUST YOU. TRUST US. THE HELMET WILL LINK YOU TO CERTAIN CIRCUITS DESIGNED FOR THIS SITUATION. WE CAN GIVE YOU NOT INFORMATION BUT KNOWLEDGE, THAT YOU WILL OBTAIN NOWHERE ELSE IN THE UNIVERSE.

"The purpose of life is to find things out," said Kin doubtfully.

YES. WHO WOULD SHUN KNOWLEDGE?

Kin sighed, reached up, grasped, pulled.

The robots were busy in the center of the deck. One of them rolled toward the horseshoe panel, trailing a cable behind it. The rest were clustered around an oddly bent piece of mirror-bright rod. When Kin looked at it her eyes ached. It seemed to be twisted in ways that normal matter just couldn't go, which meant she was looking at the heart of a matrix drive.

She was glad—she'd had a horrible thought about what would happen if one didn't get built.

The robots had also built a proper pilot's seat in front of the controls. Marco was sitting in it, swearing.

"It'll be like finding a hole in fog," he said. "I hope your tin friend builds good jets."

"The hole will show up on the screen," suggested Silver.

"Yeah. But we'll be going at a hell of a lick. Kin, are you sure it's all worked out?"

Kin smiled. "Right down to the disc's tumbling speed and the rotation of the vault of heaven. Don't you believe that machines capable of running the disc for seventy thousand years are capable of—"

"—threading a needle ten thousand miles away by dropping the thread over a *waterfall*? No. I want a chance to experiment with the jets."

"You'll have it."

The roc's wingbeats thundered in the night as it wheeled about and skimmed across the dark water. It dropped the ship, fought frantically for height again, wingtips brushing the waves.

There was a moment of free-fall, then a slap as the ship hit. It bobbed, and spun slowly.

The roc passed across the stars, wings booming, heading back to its secret valleys. And Kin relaxed. Through the hull of the ship there came a new sound, a soft murmur as of distant engines. The rimfall.

She waited, with the soft padding of the helmet pressing against her closed eyes. Nothing happened.

Then she *remembered.* It came as a shock, but that dwindled as She took control over the body. How could She have forgotten? Then She remembered about that, too. Unless One forgot, how could One learn?

She could feel Kin somewhere in Her mind, a little flask of tastes and textures, senses and experiences. Around Her She could experience the disc, and she knew there was danger there. It would be too easy to lose herself in the sheer exhilarating enjoyment of it. She turned her mind back to the computers.

You have done well.

THAT WAS MY TASK.

I will allow some recollection to Kin Arad. She is Me, after all. She will awake knowing something about Us. And she will understand about the disc.

YES.

She reached into the mind within Her and made certain amendments. Then, contented, She let Herself forget. . . .

Kin remembered. The memories were there, cold, hard, real, like shards of ice in the mind. She recalled the disc.

"The disc," she said, her voice flat in the shock of it, "is the boot in the coal measure, the coin in the crystal. The filling in the tooth of the triceratops. The secret mark that reveals the maker. They couldn't resist it. They built a perfect universe to specifications, but they couldn't resist adding the disc out here, hard to find, but a clue. *How do I know?*" she shouted.

The screen stayed blank.

"I *know* it. They weren't just the disc builders. They built the lot—the real Earth, Kung, all the stars. They laid down our fossils. We thought maybe the Great Spindle Kings had done that, but the Spindle Kings never existed.

They were all part of the false strata of the new universe. We wondered if we'd evolved with the help of the Kings. We never evolved! We were created, just as we recreate whales and elephants for our colony worlds.

"We're a colony universe. The Builders just moved in and built it, and because everyone needs a history, they gave us a history. Just as we do with the new worlds. Ancient bones. Fabulous monsters. Great Spindle Kings, Wheelers. And we never realized it. We did it ourselves, and we never tumbled to it.

"Then one of them built the disc. Almost as a joke, maybe? Certainly for no important reason. An exercise in ingenuity. It must have been an afterthought, a collection of neat ideas, put together after the main work was done.

"Seventy thousand years! That's the age of the universe—it's hardly got its paint scratched! We thought it was four billion years old. The *evidence* said that it was, and we believed in the evidence."

She leaned back. She could still feel the memories there, like old facts forgotten until now. She probed them gingerly, as a tongue explores a hollow tooth.

"Old. Intelligent. Divorced from matter. That's how I remember the Builders. Each one bigger than we can imagine, or maybe smaller, because—because there would be nothing to measure, except the ego. I said old? Even their age couldn't be measured, because until they built the universe there was no time. Am I right?"

WE CANNOT ANSWER THAT QUESTION BRIEFLY. WE KNOW NOTHING OF THEM OTHER THAN THAT WHICH THEY TOLD US.

"What do you know of them, then?"

BEFORE THEM, THERE WAS ONLY PROBABILITY. THEY IMPOSED A PATTERN ON THAT PROBABILITY.

"Why?"

YOUR COMPANY BUILDS WORLDS. THERE IS NO REAL NEED. YOUR NATAL WORLD IS NOT OVERPOPULATED. WHY?

"Once we were overpopulated. And we found that the more people there were, the more they were the same. It was the only way we could survive. People had always dreamed of a unified world. We thought it would be a richer one. It wasn't. It meant that the Eskimo got educated and learned cost accountancy, but it didn't mean that the German learned to hunt whales with a spear. It meant everyone learned how to press buttons, and no one remembered how to dive for pearls.

"Then the Mindquakes got us. That would have been—yes, a couple of years after the Terminus probes. People just died. Died in their billions, too, their minds just kind of folded in on themselves.

"Afterward, we had to start over. At least we had all the toys of the Spindle Kings to play with, and we could spread out—we had to spread out, after the Quakes. They made us look hard for mental elbow room, new worlds where we could flee and learn the forgotten ways. We had built robots to remember some of them for us!

"We thought it was natural, a trodden path. You see, we had the example of the Spindle Kings. We thought that any intelligent species filled its home world until the sheer mind pressure started killing them off, and then the survivors embarked on interstellar colonization; whatever way they rationalized it, the real reason would be a fierce desire to escape from other people. And then, since usable worlds aren't that common, they'd start to learn planetary engineering. Oh, we had it all carefully calculated. Race after race, fruiting and bursting across the evolving galaxy, creating new worlds before they died and in the process making new seedbeds for new races. I wrote a book about it, called *Continuous Creation*. Ha ha."

NOW YOU CAN WRITE THE SECOND EDITION.

"It'll be a bit short, I'm damn sure about that. What can I say? 'The lights in the sky are scenery'?"

WHY NOT?

"You haven't told me why the—Builders built."

The words flashed on to the screen immediately, as if the computers had been preparing them.

HUMANS ARE INQUISITIVE. THAT IS A FUNCTION OF THEIR HUMANITY. THE BEINGS THAT BUILT THIS UNIVERSE DID SO BECAUSE IT WAS UNTHINKABLE THAT THEY SHOULD NOT. CREATION IS NOT A THING THAT GODS DO, IT IS SOMETHING THAT THEY ARE.

"And afterward? What did they do next?"

There was white water around the ship. Kin could see a little tree-shrouded island beyond one port, a humped black shape in the twilight, and could feel the hull bouncing over the water.

The sky wheeled. There was no jolt, it was simply that

now the floor was just a wall. Foam covered the ports for a moment, and then Kin could look—down.

The rimfall hung before them, looking exactly like a luminous white road. Marco in the pilot's seat was outlined against it, and Kin could see that he had instinctively braced himself with his feet scrabbling for a hold.

Down, way down, there was a ball of fire in the sky. The disc was in darkness now, but the little orbiting sun was giving a brief day to the face of the waterfall. While Kin watched, it climbed above her and disappeared as the ship overtook it.

Later there was a cloud at the limit of vision. It stayed there for a while, then raced up the glittering stream at a speed that made Kin flinch. There was the faintest of lurches and a second's darkness as the ship left the water behind at the molecule sieve, and then there were stars.

There was a long hiss from Marco. It may have been a sigh of relief.

Silver said, "I would have felt happier if the computers had been able to arrange a more conventional launching, but I must admit that it had style."

"From their point of view this was the most efficient way," said Kin. The sky spun again as Marco turned the ship so that "down" was where long tradition had always put it, in the region of the feet.

Silver unfastened her couch straps, then looked across at Kin.

"We built the universe, didn't we?" she said. "Not *us* precisely, these lumps of bone and brain, but the thing in us that makes us what we are. The thing that dreams while the rest of us is asleep."

Kin smiled. "The computers wouldn't tell," she said. "But yes, you're right. I think the computers had a certain extra function; they could suppress all the mental static so the—oh hell, why avoid the world?—so that the god inside could surface just for a while and perform. That's why practically anyone could be the disc master. If Jago Jalo had tried the helmet, he'd be there still."

"No one will believe you," said Marco, without turning his head.

"I'm not sure that would be a tragedy," said Kin. "The disc was put there as a hoax, or a hint. No one has to believe it. We'll build a planet for the disc people and transfer them, and that is the thing that needs to be done."

The challenge warmed her. The building of a new Earth; so carefully done that the disc people could be transferred and not know it. There'd have to be new continents designed, and the disc people would have to be put into a freeze-sleep until some of their number had bred enough to populate them. It could take a thousand years. There'd be a whole solar system to drag into place, great planets around far stars to be ringed in some vast fields and flipped across light-years.

Buffaloes to be designed.

Life wouldn't be boring.

Would what the computers could tell them pay for it?

It would.

They slept and they ate, while the ship dipped under the monstrous shadow in the sky. The little toiling sun shed no light on the blackness as it swung across it.

Presently the far edge of the rimfall began to grow larger. Marco slid back into his seat and spoke to the ship's little brain.

"Okay," he reported, "major burn coming up. This is where we say goodbye, so get into those couches. The Committee is timing this one for us."

It took ten minutes of slight discomfort, listening to the faint roar from the outrigger jets. Kin heard a sigh from Marco's couch as the engines shut off.

"That's it," he said. "Now we hit the hole, or we miss the hole. I never thought I'd have to worry about running into the wall of the universe."

The rimfall raced past a few thousand miles away, phosphorescent in the light of the full moon. Even Marco took a deep breath as the ship rose above the edge of the disc and plunged toward the sky.

The disc was a design of white and black, a silver-and-ebony coin floating under a sky wild with stars.

The stars were getting nearer. The moon became a pearl hovering over the disc, and the stars were *definitely* getting nearer.

The hole that Jago Jalo had cut in the vault of heaven had been big enough for the ring ship to go through, and this one was much smaller. But it would be approaching it at a low angle.

The computers had told Marco that the hole would be wide enough. They had told Kin the same, but had added their estimate of the distance to spare. Kin hadn't dared pass it on to Marco. The minimum clearance was a little less than a meter.

She found she was staring ahead, searching the sky. The other two were doing the same. Stars were drifting overhead. While Kin watched, their silent, snowflake movement became a brisk race.

Then they were a blur. There was the briefest impression of something around the ship as a star swelled, blazed and disappeared. A slight shudder marked the demise of one of the outrigger jets, knocked off against the edge of the sky.

Then there were stars again, deceptively similar, and the ship was dropping into the gulf.

She could hear Marco breathing noisily. Silver was humming a tune in a rolling baritone.

Kin watched the stars she knew were only seventy thousand years old, marginally older than their cousins hanging from the vault of heaven. Stars were just lights in the sky, but bigger skies demanded bigger stars.

Kin thought about the second edition. The ship fell onward into the scenery.

ABOUT THE AUTHOR

Terry Pratchett had his first story published when he was aged thirteen (in *Science Fantasy*); his first full-length book, *The Carpet People,* was finished when he was eighteen, and published when he was twenty. *The Dark Side of the Sun* was published in 1976, and he has written many shorter s.f. stories.

He lives with his wife and daughter in Somerset and now describes himself as a Drop-In, one of a (growing?) number of people who have forsaken the rural rat race for the Good Life—which, he says, *really* comprises warm rooms and not having to dig your own potatoes. "It was hard work being a peasant," he says. "All that rivalry over who has got the sharpest scythe and the most efficient woodburning stove quite got me down."

He now works for the Central Electricity Generating Board, keeps bees, mucks around with electronics and enjoys life.

RoC
SF
ADVANCE